THE LAWS OF ENTANGLEMENT

A TRUE LOVE STORY

MAYA PREISLER

MOCHA MEMOIRS PRESS

Published by Mocha Memoirs Press, LLC
ISBN 978-0-9998522-8-6

Credits:

Cover art: Maya Preisler
Editors: Ria Preisler Rabun
Danae Whitaker
Proofreader: Novellette Whyte

For Raven: 因为你，此书得以存在。
冇辦法用言語嚟形容我對你嘅愛。

ACKNOWLEDGMENTS

Acknowledgements: Raising a book — much like a child or a barn — requires a village. First and foremost, my deepest gratitude and acknowledgements to my sister, Ria for being the best sister, friend, editor, and co-conspirator I could ask for. Thank you, little sister. Without you, I wouldn't even be alive, much less writing. A large part of my writing skill is due to your tireless and patient feedback over the past twenty years. I must also thank my High School English teachers: Mrs. Munns and Ms. Craven. I owe almost everything I know about writing to them. Thank you both for believing in me. This book would not have happened without your patient guidance and difficult assignments. Thank you to my friend and publisher, Nicole Givens Kurtz, for encouraging a baby writer to take her first scary steps into the professional writing world. Thank you, boss. I'll try to be a good Jane. Thank you to my soul sisters and beta readers for their valuable feedback

— Tamara, Wen-Jie, and Lily — thank you for your encouragement and support, especially when I was terrified. And finally, thank you to my ineffable, indelible, red-thread Star Family. Each of you is a piece of my heart.

OTHER MOCHA MEMOIRS
PARANORMAL ROMANCE TITLES

PROLOGUE

A WISE MAN once said that love teaches you about yourself. Of course, he was right. Love taught me how to feel, how to be happy, how to communicate. Love taught me to live in mindful appreciation of each moment. Love taught me I was someone worth loving, that I was capable of more than I had ever imagined. Love taught me how to value myself.

In the beginning, I thought I had been cursed by a cruel universe intent on savouring my suffering. I thought love was a punishment for some past crime and my circumstances doomed me to trauma. I thought I was a victim. The most important lesson I learned from love was that life is a result of how you see the universe, not how the universe sees you. Love taught me to reclaim my power. Love taught me I was a hero. In following my heart, I learned to reshape my perspective, my life, and — ultimately — the world.

This is the story of how love saved my life.

1

My soulmate was already dead the first time we met. My sister had specifically warned me away from falling in love with him, but forbidden fruit has always promised to be much sweeter. Her warning only served to make him more appealing. I was riveted by the record of his life, drawn inexorably to the timeless wisdom he possessed. He knew cosmic truths I did not, and this gnostic thirst gave me the courage to seek him.

Uncertain in my womanhood, I knew my worth as a student. Surely he would take me as a pupil.

I undertook my journey with great care, endeavouring to ensure my safety having taken the necessary precautions. Going astral allowed me to take my shields and protections with me, leaving my body guarded and anchored for safekeeping. Honestly, astral projection helps me focus. If you are going to bargain with the dead, you *must* be in control.

I sat cross-legged on a worn, wooden floor. Incense

filled the air, sweet rich coils snaking around folding screens partitioning off the rest of the room. Raven sat across from me, his effortless posture proclaiming he was far more comfortable with the pose. While my knees and thighs stuck up awkwardly from the floor at acute angles, his knees gently hugged the floor with his feet folded beneath him. I slouched, shoulders rounded in a self-conscious attempt to disguise my breasts. He sat straight and tall, his broad shoulders forming a strong horizontal line.

I couldn't help but stare in ardent appreciation. He possessed a form made to be worshipped; lips to be kissed, strong sculpted shoulders for holding, hazel-green eyes with the power to hypnotize. His perfect posture and poise reminded me of a serene, meditating Buddha statue, the black of his outfit somber against his tawny beige skin. I tried not to panic; social skills were not my strong suit, and I struggled when faced with such a sublime specimen. His death was a shame.

The palms of my small hands were sweaty, my stomach contorting in acrobatic somersaults. Physical sensations are often a component of the astral experience. All sensations arise in the mind. Your mind does not differentiate between sensory data collected in the realm of the living and data collected elsewhere. All mortal experience is the result of extended hallucinations, a complex audio-visual projection originating in experience.

Heart pounding, pulse racing, I struggled to breathe, crushed by rising pressure. In my room, talking to him had seemed so easy. Confronted with him here, I was suddenly terrified by the inescapable sensation we were tethered together by an invisible force. The gravitational pull was a tangible and indisputable law of physics, paralyzing in its implications. This encounter had already changed me, and I was only beginning to realize the scope of those changes.

"Thank you for agreeing to meet with me."

Without warning, he leaned forward and kissed me.

A palpable current arced up from my lips over the crest of my skull, running down my back in droplets as goosebumps blossomed on my skin. My entire being was a single electron jumping into a higher energy orbit. For a moment, I existed beyond all space and time. My awareness narrowed to the singularity of his kiss, surpassing conscious thought. I was no longer certain my stomach was part of my body, having rapidly ascended from the floorless abyss to this new, precarious height. I was still sitting stunned when he apologized.

"I'm sorry." An expression of earnest worry drew down his thick dark brows, causing wrinkles to form on his high forehead.

I couldn't comprehend his reasoning. "Why are you apologizing?"

"I should have asked first." His face was the picture of innocence, eyes wide with regret, devoid of guile. I found his unguarded integrity even more appealing than his chiselled face and sculpted body.

"I'll forgive you, if you do it again." Emboldened by the first kiss, I wanted another. The mysterious force drawing me to him demanded more. This craving was an irrational compulsion unlike anything I had ever known. My urge to explore these sensations passed beyond the limits of desire and far into the realms of need. I was a being of electricity — a subatomic particle accelerating vibrationally; a ringing sound filled my ears and the rich, heady scent of incense filled my nose. His hair was soft and curly in my hands. When we kissed, he tipped my chin with his hand, as though I were a precious flower. I don't remember what we spoke of that day; only the wonder of our shared connection and the hours we spent simply holding hands remains. Our first kiss is a memory I visit often; one I keep in a vault for rainy days when all seems lost.

Of all the things you might be prepared for a spirit to do, nothing prepares you for them falling in love with you.

————

THERE EXISTED a time when I was so fatigued from the constant pain of missing him I buckled under the colossal mass of my grief. I became the statue of Atlas, back bent from the weight of the world. Nearly twenty years in, I surrendered to the consensus of the masses: he was dead and I needed to move on.

I became embittered and exhausted, tired of trying to trick a tyrannical reality into giving me my greatest wish: a life lived in the light of his love. My grandparents were dead or dying, and I felt the familial *giri* to produce the next generation falling on my shoulders. The shared mythology of popular culture had taught me my worth as a woman rested solely upon my ability to procure a mate and procreate, preferably at a young age. Society's appraisal of my value was missing a core component: I was in my thirties and still single. My sister and closest friends were married, with the exception of one, committed to a life of single blessedness. Mortality stretched out before me, the need to build a foundation of family mounting with each passing day. One of my younger brothers was already a father. Watching the baby I raised create a family of his own made me feel I was a time-traveling grandmother. These pressures combined with the ever-present ache of longing to make a potent potion of "pragmatism."

My immature dream of loving a dead man belonged with my stuffed E.T., baby brush, and high school yearbooks; it was a childhood relic best placed in a storage box and forgotten. The pain of loving him had grown too great, had come perilously close to destroying me. I had sworn to never let the pain break me, but my oath was wearing thin around the edges, red threads disintegrating slowly with the painful passage of time. In my deepest moments of weakness I knew if his spirit beckoned me into the next world, I would leave this life without a second thought. I resolved, however, that there was so much more to experience in life than waiting for him.

I placed my hands between us, pushing Raven away. "I don't think this is a good idea anymore."

"What?" His amber brown eyes were full of pain and betrayal, narrow brows drawn into a sharp crease at the centre of his forehead.

My heart was a singularity, a blackened ember too dim to produce light, only capable of collapsing into a gravitational well. I could already feel it sucking the centre of my soul inward in endless spaghettification, smothering the flames that burned there. "I can't do this anymore. I can't spend the rest of my life waiting for you. I'm sorry. It's too much."

His lower lip quivered slightly, liquid pooling in his eyes as he reached for me. The fine elven features of his face were distorted into a mask of pain, his grimace a grappling hook embedded in my intestines, slowly twisting them into painful knots. "After all this?"

He was right. I was a terrible person for walking away from him after all we had been through. After all he had done for me and given to me, I was repaying his endless love and loyalty with a spectacular betrayal beyond the ken of most mortal men. I hated myself for doing this, and I knew I always would.

"I love you, Raven. I always will. But you're not here; you aren't real. None of this is." I stepped out of his reach. My willpower was a soap bubble; if he touched me, my conviction would burst. Weeks of agonizing analysis had brought me to this heartrending conclusion. A surge of tears threatened to overflow the floodwalls of my eyelids, each a sharp shard of broken glass. The singularity in my chest was collapsing, making it hard to breathe. I turned away from him and began walking into the mist.

"Kara..." the pain of his mournful plea was even heavier than my own sorrow.

Still, I walked.

Every step from him was torture. I longed to turn around and run back into his arms and wrap myself in his embrace. Even if he *was* a *tulpa*, surely having a thought-form to love was better than having nothing at all. I considered abandoning my course, but instead I sharpened my resolve. Only by refusing to acknowledge his presence could I dismiss the delusion I had created and return it to the shapeless ether from which I had unconsciously formed it. I could still feel him behind me, the force anchoring me to him stretching painfully with every step. I expected the tether to suddenly snap — a rubber band pushed past its limits. No matter how far I travelled, the tension remained.

The ache in my chest intensified; the need to return to his orbit a painfully persistent demand in my core. I trudged forward, each breath an agony, deliberately choosing to ignore the clarion call of my soul ringing out behind me. I was certain the black hole of my heart had swallowed me. Who I had been was dying, pulled down into formless oblivion. I continued walking.

Beyond the periphery of pain lurked a world full of promise: flowers bloomed, lightning struck, sunsets glowed, planets danced, and the universe begged to be known. I wanted to *live*, to explore, to experience the wonders awaiting me. I focused on the tangible aspects of my life: pursuing my passions, building a business, paying the bills.

Mundane life occupied with the necessities of career and cash, my lifelong passion for magic still called to me. Having progressed through the external systems available for study, I turned my gaze inward in pursuit of a more perfect self. I made a practice of investing my energy in improving myself. I took online classes and seminars, read books, and watched documentaries. I studied the art and science of self-improvement as though I had returned to college. This time, life itself was my professor. I dove deep into the shadowy abyss of my unconscious, seeking to repair the damage caused by a childhood of trauma.

I committed myself to the life of a monk, observing fairly strict veganism for a time. I meditated, practiced yoga, hacked my energy centres, aligned my chakras, sung mantras, and embarked on a strict spiritual diet of love and light. I said affirmations in the mirror, changed my language, and made a short film as a visualization aid — overachievers never settle for simple things like vision boards. Ultimately, all my sugary-sweet positivity was only theatre backdrop. Backstage, I still suffered.

My dogged pursuit of a life comprised only of love and light proved shallow and short-sighted. This myopic focus hid the real truth: deep inside I held a core wound which was killing me. Unbearable torment was my deepest secret, the one I tried to hide from everyone. Try as I might to release the dream of a life lived in his laughter, I could not escape the gravitational force pulling me into Raven's orbit. The need to be near him was an inherent part of my being and informed much of who I was. As much as my conscious mind perceived the denial of my desire for him as a spiritual act of self-compassion, it created a burden I had unconsciously chosen. If I couldn't be with him, I would carry his loss with me in an endless act of self-flagellation.

2

MY IDENTITY OF TRAGIC LOVER, the poor Juliet left
alive, was so strong I inadvertently summoned others
who bore wounds of love to my side. Like moths to a
flame, the lost, lonely, and pathetic found me — the
princess of existential angst. These people were invari-
ably the same: broken little boys and girls with sharp
facades of power, either in their pretentiousness or their
pitiableness. They seized upon me as virgins upon a
unicorn, convinced by the strength of my sadness that I
was the source they had been seeking. They thought
two broken halves could be combined into a whole, that
their own fractured hearts would be sufficient to repair
mine. They were wrong. I found their fascination with
me so frustrating I wrote a poem about it: *And I who have
tasted ambrosia, how could mere honey ever sate these lips?*
That poem was my mantra when dealing with them and
their nice guy™ entitlement for years. However, some-

times their insight wounded me — as with the self-professed priest of the Tuatha De Dannan.

He arrived in my life like the flu, brought home through contact with others. I attended a local coven's Wicca 101 class to ascertain whether or not an association with their group would be worth pursuing. Accompanied by my usual coterie of young, pagan college kids, I followed the flyer to the bookstore. We entered through the café doors and wound our way through the tables to the velvet roped line, waiting our turns to order. Last of our group, I ordered my customary Irish crème Italian soda and paid the barista, turning to find Emma waiting for me. The others had gone ahead.

We found them near the metaphysical section, where padded wooden chairs had been arranged in two concentric half circles around some coffee tables. Jon and Gwen had already taken seats in the front row, saving space for Emma and me next to them. I wished they had chosen seats in the second row, but it was too late now to change our arrangements. Other latecomers were behind us, taking their seats in the back. With an inward sigh, I slid into the chair next to Emma. Drinks in hand, we listened to an introductory lecture on ritual tools, which had already begun before our arrival.

"This is a cauldron, the customary tool for Earth." A tall woman with long blonde hair waved her pale pink hands over a heavy metal cauldron set in the centre of the table.

Or Fire. Or Spirit. Or even Water. And what about the dish or the pentacle? Aren't you leaving some things out, lady? I was frustrated by the incomplete information this priestess was parcelling out to her audience, as if magic were a ready-to-wear off-the-rack Halloween costume instead of custom-made Renaissance garb. Even in Wicca, that simply wasn't true; there are as many paths as there are people. This fact is *supposed* to be one of the reasons for practicing the craft. Pagans are *supposed* to be like Libertarian Protestants, creating their own relationships with the divine without intermediaries or authorities.

"And this is the sword, the customary tool for Air. Now this confuses a lot of people…" She smiled with the air of a condescending kindergarten teacher. I ground my teeth and tried not to growl under my breath.

Here comes the wands are for fire and swords are for air argument, ripped straight out of the pages of the Rider Waite Tarot deck. I struggled to resist the urge to roll my eyes.

The priestess continued, "Now this often confuses most beginners…"

"Most people are too ignorant to realize swords are a tool of the will." A slick, oily voice broke into the conversation, its owner rising as he spoke. A pale, scrawny white man with greasy hair the colour of dirty dishwater stepped up to the table, pushing the priestess away from her invisible podium. I wondered how she would respond to this interruption. Misinformation or withholding secrets from neonates is a tradition as old as the craft. If she exerted her authority and reminded him of his place, I would know she was truly a priestess and only dissembling for show. The bookstore was a public place, after all.

"The sword is sharp and possesses the ability to cut,

like wit," he continued. Defeated, the priestess sighed and took a seat. *Not a real priestess then, and probably also genuinely ignorant.*

I surreptitiously looked around to gauge the responses of the people around me. Several were nodding as though the utter garbage spewing forth from this man's mouth were divine wisdom. *What the hell is wrong with these people? Do they not realize that swords are born from flames? They are creatures of death and destruction, violence and change. Wands came from trees, trees which breathe out oxygen that we in turn inhale as air. Trees are the ancient keepers of wisdom, not warlords. I am surrounded by idiots.*

"I see that some of you aren't recognizing the truth behind these symbols." He spoke patiently, tilting his narrow head to the side and smiling with a level of condescension that made the priestess's seem kind by comparison. "During the 'Burning Times,' it was important to keep many of our symbols secret. Certain symbols were changed and reversed so the mysteries could be kept safe. Any commoner would have said wands were tools of air, and therefore would not be an initiate. Only a student of the will would know the truth." His thin lips stretched even further in a garrulous smile, a garish imitation of the Cheshire Cat.

Really? They changed the symbols to something that does *make sense to keep the secrets safe? What?! Don't you idiots realize he has this backwards? Isn't anyone going to question him? Look at this guy. He's a caricature of a used-car salesman. Come on!*

To be fair, I had already attained the full degree

requirements to become clergy in their religion and so found myself an elder while so recently a child. I had been raised with magic and spirits, studying the arcane arts my whole life. While the audience (my friends included) were easily enthralled by this charismatic flimflam man who quickly hijacked the lecture with his grandstanding, I knew better. I knew he was lying. My friends, however, were sold; they took him back to campus with us, to perform a séance in the dorm. None of them knew I was a medium.

"This blanket…" he nearly purred while he stroked the crocheted afghan Emma kept in the chair across from her bed. His eyes were focused on hers, watching her face for any flicker of emotion. *I see you, liar. You're not reading the blanket. You're reading* **her**.

"This blanket was made by someone close to you… a female… yes, an older woman." He stretched his sentences out slower than William Shatner in a Priceline™ commercial, until he was speaking at sloth speed. *It's crocheted. Of course it was made by someone close to her. And of course it was made by an older woman. You don't need psychic talents to figure that out — Sherlock Holmes would have guessed as much immediately upon entering the room.* I sighed and rolled my eyes. *I'm surrounded by idiots.*

"She's passed, but I can feel her presence here with us now." His voice was even slimier than it had been at the bookstore, persuasion and guile oozing out of every pore.

I surreptitiously checked the room for ghosts. Other than the living, the room was empty. *Ghosts: zero. Charlatans: one.*

"She is short and a little chubby; she looks a bit like you." *Lucky guess, asshole. I look like my grandmother too.* I ground my teeth and sighed again.

He continued, dazzling them with his showmanship. His charade was both incredibly painful and hilarious to me, largely comprised of leading questions used in stage magic, complete with misdirection and guesswork. As soon as he left the dorm, I told them as much.

"You aren't really helping the 'New Age practitioners are all idiots' stereotype, you know." I flopped down on the spare bottom bunk and rolled my eyes.

"What are you talking about?" Jon shoved his ecru hands in his pockets and frowned.

"I'm talking about you three morons falling for the simplest and oldest of cons. You're lucky he was only seeking attention and power, not money."

"But he..." Emma began, shaking her dark head.

"But he what? Walked into a dorm room and picked out the only handmade object in here and assumed any teenager who brought something sentimental from home would have a deep emotional attachment to said object? And then proceeded to make a series of logical deductions based upon the statistical probability of their success? Old woman make blankets, especially if they're knit or crocheted. And everyone looks like their grandmother."

"So why Emma?" Gwen narrowed her eyes, placing her hands on her narrow hips.

"Your bear is in the top bunk where he couldn't see it. The afghan is sitting out in the open where you see it upon first entering the room. Plus, you're not as pretty as Emma. And you read as butch."

"I'm not an abomination! I would never!" Gwen glared at me, her pale pink skin quickly turning red.

"I know," I acknowledged her disagreement with a dismissive wave of my hand. *Me thinkest thou dost protest too much. Homophobia always leads back to people who are afraid of themselves.* "You and Jon also entered together and could be perceived as a couple. Emma is a chubby virgin with a need to be loved. He's a creepy old white guy trying to take advantage of young pagan girls. He was watching Emma like a predator the entire time, gauging her reactions. He's looking for a group of young pagans to lead so he can sleep with initiates. Don't you guys know about the local coven's Priest who was arrested for sex with a twelve-year-old? Or the local ritual where the Maiden was a fourteen-year-old and the Horned God a fifty-year-old? Or the cult leaders at the coast who tricked young girls into having group orgies? Paganism is as full of sexual predators seeking children as the publishing industry is."

Two weeks later, he appeared at my house. I came home for the summer to find him in my living room, eating cookies and drinking tea, a pale, preening peacock perched on a dark green leather sofa. I narrowed my eyes at his scrawny white form, suppressing a growl. This was *my* house. What was he doing here?

"What are you doing here?" I stood with my hands on my abundant hips, legs spaced at the ready, in the perfect fighting stance.

"I came to invite you to join me. I've heard your coven needs a priest. And *I* need a priestess." The heat of his roving eyes was unbearable and nauseating.

"I have no idea what you're talking about." *What kind of witch was he to say such things!?* Maintaining secrecy about our working partners was part of the path. You *never* outed anyone else from the proverbial broom closet. This rule was a cultural relic of the Inquisition and not lightly broken. In the not so distant past, sharing this knowledge resulted in death. *Deny everything.*

He stood, walking toward me. I was grateful my back was to the door, which lay open behind me. Although I was not one for retreating, I would not be trapped. He was undeniably creepy; an albino peacock strutting awkwardly in a garish display of gaudy feathers. Waves of false desire radiated from him as he tried to use his glamour to entrap me. "I am the Priest of Don and Danu. Be my Priestess. Embrace your power." He pushed his aura towards me in sickening pulses of lust and greed.

"No." My hackles rose at the mere mention of those names.

"You're wasting your time, you know. The one you're waiting for, you'll never find him. Join me." He stepped toward me again, opening his hand in a gesture of welcome.

I nearly gagged on the scent of his cloying staleness. I stepped back through the door, holding the door open for him from the outside.

"Get out of my house. Now." The voice of command

rang in my head. If he could use his will to push at mine, I could do the same. Bolstered by panic and anger, my power overcame his, forcing him to leave the boundaries of my property. I double-locked the front door, pressing my high forehead against the cold metal while I took deep, cleansing breaths to clear the adrenaline, cortisol, and norepinephrine from my system.

Despite my anger, his words haunted me. He saw through my façade, straight into the core of my being and told me my worst fear would come true. Was it another of his stage acts? A last attempt to persuade me? The truth? The seed of doubt was planted.

After him, the self-professed messenger of "The Council" — the supposed reincarnation of Imhotep — appeared. His narcissistic attempts to destroy my world were more direct than the last pretender.

"You're hung up on a dead guy, so that you don't have to be threatened with the risk of dating the living. The next time you fall in love with someone, check for a heartbeat first." The cruel tone of his voice told me he thought I was a lesser life form unworthy to be in his presence.

Despite confessing his intention to sunder my relationship with my sister, Rhiannon, his words still held some kind of power over me. Even after he had addicted my best friend to crack and run off to New York to be a famous film producer, I still wondered if his cutting remark could be correct.

When the third cocksure, charismatic sociopath arrived in my life, my inner doubts and chronically low self-esteem had reduced me to a low-hanging fruit ripe for the picking. I was riddled with insecurities, and his love-bombing found ample purchase to sink in, tooth and claw. Drunk on the promise of finally having found love, I subsumed myself into his world. He was a nuclear explosion; ionizing radiation stripping away my subatomic structure electron by electron, eroding and reshaping me until I was fully isolated and in his thrall. Despite societal approval and the success of having finally found someone bolstering my ego, I secretly knew something was wrong. I lay awake nights listening to him sleep next to me, painfully aware the black hole I held hidden in my heart remained unfilled. In a way, this awareness was a blessing. When my usefulness as a decoration to pacify his ego had faded and life became a tsunami of toxicity, this knowledge saved me.

3

I REMEMBER the end of our relationship clearly. I lay awake in his bed. Locking the door hadn't mattered; he had retreated to the downstairs den and the comfort of his media centre after our fight ended. He obviously planned to sleep down there. Some part of me, however, needed the door to be locked. Subconsciously, I didn't trust him not to come upstairs and harm me in my sleep. He never thought twice before using my sleeping body to satiate his lust; I doubted he would pause before satisfying his anger either. I was infuriated over the idea of going to bed without resolving anything. I couldn't believe he would walk away and refuse to talk about what had happened between us. I was also secretly relieved. If I was honest with myself, talking hadn't done any good this time and never had any of the times before.

My mind kept slipping back to the scene which had played out only a few short hours before. I stood at the stove, cooking dinner, as always. My heart was already heavy, having recently hung up the phone from our argument. "My passion for you and this relationship is gone," he had said, as though love was a mysterious force, a fog that evaporated under prolonged sunlight. I couldn't understand his statement or even the concept. In my world, love was a permanently life-altering force as inexorable as gravity. Such a powerful feeling simply disappearing overnight was unfath-omable to me. I was busy trying not to season the skillet with the salt of my tears when he entered, ranting about an NPR segment he'd heard on the drive home.

With horror, I listened as he spewed racist rhetoric, filled with vitriol for what he saw as the entitlement of others. Armed with facts and figures drawn from my liberal college education, I shot down his arguments with military precision. All he could see was red. The more I questioned his self-centric worldview, the more of an enemy I became. Eventually, I found myself seated at the round kitchen table, backed into the corner of the room with no ready escape. He stood on the other side of the wooden surface, waving his muscular arms and shouting madly. I spoke in even, measured tones, trying to calm him.

But the anger in his voice would not be sated — he wanted blood. Terrified by the threat of violence in his eyes, I bargained for my safety with the oldest and last resort of the battered. "I love you..." I began, pleadingly.

"Do you?!?" He gesticulated with his pale pink

arms in a perfect imitation of a demented car lot blow up doll. "I'm the man! The white man!"

I lay awake, sick with self-analysis and resulting realization. How had I come to be here in this place, with this person? How had such a monster convinced me he was a hero? Had I ever known him at all? Had he ever known me? Lines from Jeanette Winterson's *Sexing the Cherry*, which I had first read a lifetime ago as a teenager, appeared unbidden in my head.

Suddenly the enchanted city fades and you are left alone again in the windy desert. As for your beloved, she didn't understand you.

The truth is, you never understood yourself.[1]

The familiar passage took on new meaning in this revelation of age. Had I ever known myself? Hot, fresh tears of shame washed down my cheeks. I had hidden all I truly was behind my need to be desirable. I remembered the agony of my initial text conversations with him: the many times I would write, erase, and rewrite each word under the scrutinizing eye of my inner critic. How could he have ever known me? I had never given him the opportunity. We had been too busy hiding our vulnerability behind masks of perfection. When the masks fell off, we were appalled at what lay underneath. The price of subsuming myself to what I thought I should want was waking up to someone so anathema to who I truly was I felt terrified of him. He was right; I didn't love the real him — I couldn't. I had nearly married a monster, the sort who would have used our children as weapons against me, while arguing that the genetic inferiority they inherited from their mixed mother made them less than he. The raw horror of this thought transported me back in time to a memory I had forgotten.

———

WE — Rhiannon, Rainbow, Three Moons, and I — sat in a silver van parked across the street from an all too familiar house. Two of my companions stood sentry, keeping an eye out for both partygoers and trouble. I don't remember what my friends were doing; I was too lost in thought, reliving my past with the house. I loved every inch of its nineteenth century boards, from the formerly detached kitchen to the sweeping front staircase. The house was a hot haunted mess, populated by a variety of hungry dead. One of them, a little girl, had once pushed me down those front stairs after I banned her from my room. My ankle still occasionally ached from the break. I was not here for her tonight, or for the patient waiting for Doctor Aiken, who had added onto this house in the early twentieth century, transforming it into his home and medical practice. I was here for my friend.

The local "burner" population cavorted in the backyard, their raucous cries of mourning a strange cross between Mad Max and an Irish wake. We were all here for her tonight. I could see her, wandering the outskirts of the crowd listlessly, her height making her easily visible from a distance. My heart ached at the sight of her. Suicides always make you hurt when you look at them, but watching someone you love carry around so much heartbreak is devastating. I swallowed, praying for the strength to complete this task.

Helping suicides pass over is never easy. If they have a Master ghost trapping them among the living, guiding them to the place of passage is even more difficult. Master ghosts derive their power from the suffering of those under their unearthly thrall. They are as likely to allow a medium to assist one of their herd into making passage as an addict is to give up their stash. Arranging escape for Makayla would be an arduous challenge, but I *had* to do it. I believed her death was partially my fault. If I couldn't help a friend in need, what kind of medium was I?

Everyone — besides me — had been shocked when they found Makayla dead in her bedroom. They couldn't imagine their happy friend had been so full of pain she had chosen the final solution as the best option. Few of them knew her demons; I did. I could still see us sitting at the table in the alcove of the upstairs kitchen.

"I'm worried about you, Makayla." I looked earnestly into her rich sepia eyes, pleading with all my heart. "I don't think it's safe for you to be sleeping with a Neo-Nazi. Those guys can get under your skin, destroy you from the inside. Please walk away from this before he kills you." She assured me he was harmless, her musical laughter ringing out as she shook her ebony braids from side to side.

Although she tried to deny it, I could see the damage done to her self-esteem. I was too late. Our conversation in the kitchen was the last time I saw her alive. Sitting here in this van feeling guilty wasn't going to bring her back or let her move on. I took a deep breath and went within, projecting myself into the Other.

I had grown accustomed to the miasma of the house during the two times I had lived in it, but I was unprepared for how dank it had grown in my absence. Without the care of a medium or a mage, the combination of node — the place where two leylines meet — and haunting created a powerful nexus on the Other. In the mortal realm, the house appeared beautiful but dilapidated, an unremarkable building in an historic neighbourhood on the wrong side of the redline. When my sister Rhiannon and I first found the house, it had glowed with love and promise, recently partially restored by the gentle hands of a master craftsman. The house had been so warm and bright then.

Now it was a mockery. The house had since been turned into the nerdy nice guy™ version of a frat house. Years of rape and violence wrapped in toxic masculinity and hedonism had fed the trapped energies of the past, creating a perpetual vortex of pain. The whole scene could have been lifted straight out of Beetlejuice. The angles narrowed and sharpened, distending into unnatural and unnerving forms.

The house seemed to breathe with a heavy rasp; to my senses it was a chronic smoker with COPD. Each breath brought creaks and moans, an eerie blue-green light streaming forth. I was grateful I wasn't required to go inside. I hoped that my sister's redirection of the leylines feeding the node would drain this powerhouse and allow me to influence the energy flows around the house. So long as the node was feeding the haunting, I would not be powerful enough to make a difference. I only had to stall until the draining process had begun.

I felt the house pulling me toward it, whispering to me, tempting me to step into the yard. I shook my head, planting my feet firmly in the spirit asphalt. The Goddess of Roadways and I were old friends. A tie to Her ran in my blood; all the traveling peoples are Her children. As Roma, Asphaltia long considered me Her own. My dedication to Her and creation of art in Her Name had brought Her more followers and energy. Gods tend to appreciate such things.

In the road I stood, and in the road I would stay. The safety of the road gives me a tactical advantage and I use it whenever possible. My plan involved getting my friend to come to me. *How do I draw Makayla's attention in such a way as to not advertise my presence to everything else in a three-mile radius of the house?*

As luck would have it, she began drifting my way. I waved and called her name, hoping those actions alone would be enough to bring her to me. If she thought herself at the party, coming over to say hello to an old friend would fit perfectly into her reality. I didn't want to frighten her, especially if she didn't realize she was dead. A face I recognized from my nightmares and the memory of shapes outside my window at night appeared over her shoulder: the creeper. He wrapped his arms around her possessively and whispered in her ear. His ghostly corpse grey was a sharp contrast against her warm henna brown skin, and I shuddered at the thought of his cadaverous touch. He watched my face with delight, smiling as he drew her away from me. *Damnit. Damn damn damn.*

"Whatchu doin' here?" A voice rasped from behind me. I spun, startled. There was nothing. Laughter echoed down the street. *Stay cool, Riordan. Stay cool*, I told myself. *It's nothing but a spook sneaking up on you, trying to mess with your head. Pay no mind.*

"I say, whatchooo doin' here?" the voice demanded again, this time from somewhere near the house. I spun around, seeking its source. I found only more laughter. I closed my eyes, drawing strength into me from the asphalt. *Hail Asphaltia, Goddess of Roadways, Patroness of Travelers, hear me now. Protect Your child.* I went deeper, seeking Gaia. *Hail Gaia, Mother of All. Hear me. Lend me Your strength.* I could sense some *thing*, a malicious entity by the feel of it, approaching me. I hastily checked my shields for flaws, pulse quickening. The inimical spirit stood right in front of me. Feigning indifference, I opened my eyes.

He reminded me of an image out of Appalachian legend, perhaps an old-time representation of the Devil himself. My rational brain kicked into high gear, checking myths and legends to identify my unexpected conversational partner. The familiar thought process and logical analysis of facts made things less terrifying. Opening your eyes to find yourself nose to nose with a demon straight out of mountain folk tales requires some coping skills, even if you're not a believer in the two-party system. I could smell alcohol on his breath. *Could this be Old Scratch himself?*

"What you doin' here, little girl? This ain't your

kinda party. And 'sides, you got no 'thority round here anyways." He laughed, coughing excessively. Apparently demons could have smoking problems too. He and the house should try to quit together. The mental image made me laugh. He turned back to me, inhumanly quick, one tawny golden eye peering down the pale plane of that infamous hooked nose. He was so close to me that I could count each broken blood vessel in his florid snout. "What's so funny?" he demanded, all pretence at charming colloquialism gone. He was a shark whose mood had abruptly shifted upon the release of blood in the water. I tried not to shiver and to *not* imagine myself as his prey.

"I know something you do not know," I quipped, desperate for a witty answer. *Thanks, Inigo Montoya. I owe you one.*

"What is that?" He pressed his hideously huge bloodshot beak into my nose, which seemed minuscule in comparison to his. I tried not to be sick from the stench of his breath and the odious waves of greed and lust that washed out from his aura in putrid pulses.

"You have no power here either. Perhaps those who once settled these lands feared you, but no more. You're only here to feed off the debauchery and enjoy the show. You're not here to take any of these souls. You can't, or else they would have already gone with you." I filled my bluff with as much confidence as I could muster under the circumstances. My success rested entirely upon a persuasive performance of power that I did not truthfully possess.

He growled, attacking my throat with one jaundiced, clawed hand, threatening to choke me. I laughed again, speaking hoarsely through his attempt. "You can't touch me, Old Scratch. I don't belong to you. I suggest you back up, and reconsider who you're talking to." I narrowed my hazel-grey eyes — now cold steel — to small slits and met his larger feline gaze without flinching. Uncertainty took hold, and he began to back off.

"Now go back to the party and find some quality time with our friend the creeper. Or else." I deliberately stretched my full lips into a serene smile, blinking at him with feigned innocence. I hoped he couldn't tell how hard my heart was pounding.

"Or else?" he sneered.

"Or else, I'll call Kali herself to deal with you. I hear she's always hungry for demon blood."

"You wouldn't." He laughed weakly and backed up.

Silly demons, so easily played if you turned the tables of fear.

"Wouldn't I? Search the memories of the partygoers. Ask them who I am." I didn't think he could do such a thing but I knew he would never admit it. Besides, most of the males present would have a healthy amount of leftover fear and respect from the days when I ruled the house with an iron fist. They had been hunted down and killed in video games enough times to respect me, not to mention all the times I had exerted my authority and ordered them to clean up or kicked them out. Perhaps if he listened, he would hear all of the above. "This is *my* house, bitch," I spat at him in emphasis, "Check the lease." Another bluff, but I carried it off easily. The lease *might* have been rewritten by now, but as they say, the Devil is in the details.

He backed off, muttering. I looked to the node; its bright glow was starting to wane. I watched the silver tendrils of energy snake out through the leylines like the living rivers of etheric energy they were. Good. *Deep breath, Riordan. You got this.* Old Scratch was correct in one respect though: I had no authority here. None of these people worshipped my gods or kept my paths. That didn't mean I couldn't appeal to a higher authority; I merely had to find the right one. I closed my eyes, focusing on Makayla, following her energy up the soul-tree until I found a higher spark. I swallowed, praying for success in summoning the help I sought.

It is not my habit to approach gods I don't personally know. If I hadn't recognized this one, my hesitation would have stalled me altogether. Still, I paused. Calling upon Gods with whom you don't have a pre-existing relationship is similar to cold calling strangers asking for help. Sometimes you'll meet a new friend, and sometimes you'll meet someone who isn't kindly disposed toward colonizers. If I hadn't been so desperate, I might have reconsidered. But I couldn't leave my friend trapped here without trying to help her.

Would my friendship with one of Her devotees be enough to earn me Her attention? Would She be willing to speak to me? Would the small spark of African ancestry deep in my blood and heart be enough for Her to be willing to listen? My childhood Kikongo was too rusty, I would have to use English. I was not qualified to summon Her; She had mediums and priestesses of

Her own. I would have to be extremely careful and polite; Her culture was not mine. I was *just* this side of slipping down the muddy slope of cultural appropriation.

"Mamba Muntu, Mother Water, if it be Your will, please hear my prayer. I know I have no right to speak to You or to ask anything from You. Please forgive my trespasses. Dodokolo diaku. Your child needs Your help." I focused on an image of the Goddess, calling Her to mind, followed by an image of Makayla sunk in her sorrow. I felt strongly compelled to make an offering; it seemed the polite thing to do given the circumstances. I thought back to my conversations with my soul-sister, Cobra Lay-dee, about her patroness, trying to remember any details that would give me an idea for an appropriate offering.

Memory indicated that objects of value — such as rich food and drink — were most appropriate, but I had none. Supposing I had been willing to enter the property to procure refreshments from the party, any items I found would be cheap and corrupted, not to mention not truly mine to give. I also remembered that She was often gifted designer jewellery and manufactured goods. Desperately, I searched myself for something worthy.

As I flung my arms outward in frustration, the streetlight behind me glinted off the hematite star bracelet I wore. *Hail, Asphaltia. Thank You for Your wisdom.* That would do. Not only was the bracelet made of gemstones, I had worn the item for so long I knew the bracelet carried a residue of my magical energies within its stones. It was also my favourite, because of the stars. I would offer Her a piece of myself. I removed the bracelet, sliding it over freckles and trying not to pinch any arm hairs between the beads in the process. "Dodokolo diaku," I entreated Her.

I was suddenly greeted by the smell of the ocean, overwhelmed by the memory of the first time I had seen its blue expanse stretching towards the horizon, submerged in the deep and abiding love I had felt. I opened my eyes to watch Her float into the Other, the most radiantly enticing mermaid I had ever seen. Her skin was a rich, dark sepia that faded into an even darker umber and glowed with the warmth of sunset. I had never seen hands as dexterous and gracefully long as Hers. I was certain She could play any instrument with untold perfection. The sapphire blue of Her scales and the emerald green of Her serpentine companions were gemstone bright against the rich depth of Her illustrious skin. Unbound ebony curls flowed around Her on unseen currents, undulating slowly. I under- stood why tales of Her told of the devotion She inspired. She took my breath away. Her song rippled out over the sound of the party, winding its way to Makayla's ears. I saw her turn to look at the source. The relief and recognition in Makayla's eyes was enough to make me weep with joy. Watching Mother Water embrace her was the most beautiful thing I had ever seen.

———

I SURFACED from memory and returned to myself, the

marshy smell of saltwater surrounding the bed. I sat up, curious. Makayla stood at the foot of the bed, sorrow etched across her soft features. I had never been visited by someone who had crossed over. This was new.

"Makayla?"

"I've come to return the words you once gave me: Get out. Now."

4

I will shoot *anyone* once they've been bitten by a zombie. As inhuman as it may sound, doing so is an act of compassion and mercy, not to mention making solid tactical sense. At the end of the day, I am a survivor. I'll sacrifice anything for survival, even body parts. If I were bitten by the undead, I would promptly tie a tourniquet and sever the offending flesh, no questions asked. When I woke to the terrible truth that my lover was a monster, I prepared to cut out my heart. I began packing.

A corset of grief wrapped around my chest, steel boning too tight for breathing. The animal part of me longed to shred the stays and tear the torture device from my body so I could collapse into a ball and release the floodwaters rising in my eyes. But my mercenary mind agreed with Makayla — and she had said I should flee. Formed from the collective forces of childhood trauma, my mercenary mind had seen me safely to adulthood. It was to be trusted.

I shoved my sorrow down, numbing myself into a deliberate state of denial. The main benefit to having disassociation as a superpower is the ability to take decisive action in traumatic situations which would cripple most people. Future me would suffer exponentially as she unwound the coils of repressed emotion. But she would be alive to unpack — both physically and emotionally. I was willing to make that bargain.

As I packed, I was dimly aware of the echoes of my actions in the fabric of the multiverse. I could feel the ripples of my small stone spreading out into infinity, setting worlds on fire. Future possibilities and entire probability branches caught ablaze and collapsed, crumbling into dust around me. I was sick with the acrid smell of ashes and charcoal, noxious fumes making it difficult to breathe. Memories rose and fell in the flames, some burning to embers, others taking form from the smoke.

I had but a handful of precious memories, moments I treasured as evidence of his love for me. When he picked me up and carried me over a mud puddle in the woods on our first date. When he danced with me at a wedding. When he sang eighties love ballads to me in the car. I watched each event catch fire and burn, curling up around the edges the way photographs do, faces melting into flames; I watched as each happy memory was swallowed by the blazing inferno in my mind. Although the rose-coloured lenses in my glasses had cracked and fallen out months ago, my entire perspective was shattering — the dome of The Truman Show falling apart at the seams. Other memories arising in the smoke ensured their demise.

I lay in his IKEA bed, listening to the sound of him breathing next to me. Few things are lonelier than lying awake by yourself in what is supposed to be a shared bed. I had always imagined that moving in with him would be like moving in with Raven; I would fall asleep in his arms every night and awaken in them each morning. Certainly he said as much in his texts to me — how he couldn't wait to hold me in his arms every night while he slept. Yet here I was, on the other side of the bed, awake and alone. He had played on his phone before curling up with his cat, as though I was not even there. The Dust Brothers were quoting Tyler Durden in my head.

"I say, let me never be complete. I say, may I never be content. I say, deliver me from Swedish furniture. I say, deliver me from clever art. I say, evolve, and let the chips fall where they may."[1]

Tyler Durden was laughing. This entire misadventure was a suburban lie slowly stripping away my soul. I was far from content, and woefully far from complete. I could not help but compare the pathetic reality of my failed attempt at love with what I had always hoped it would be, what Raven had always been.

The swirls of soot and ashes formed into another scene. We were driving down the road, David and I. He stroked the pinkie finger of my left hand as though it were his pet, crooning in a strange voice.

"I know, Pinkie. I love you so much. I want us to be together, too."

I pulled my hand back from his and into my lap, giving him a sidelong glance from the corner of my eye. I was used to him being weird and creepy, making jokes about serial killers. This was too much.

"I guess I'll just have to cut your finger off tonight when you go to sleep, then. That way, we can be together."

Instead of breaking up with him, I sculpted him a metatarsal from white modelling clay for Valentine's Day.

Each new mirage reminded me of how long I had been watching our relationship die, how long I had seen the end coming and been afraid to act. By revealing himself to be a monster, David had done me a favour.

Even when my sister and friends arrived to help me pack and load my belongings into their vehicles, my emotional disconnection persisted. The familiar drive was a blur, as was unloading all my things. Only after everyone had gone home or to bed, leaving me alone on the living room couch, did I finally crumble. The tidal wave of emotion I had been restraining burst forth into ragged sobs. I collapsed into the bumpy weave of the brown upholstery fabric, burying my face in the cushions to scream.

The flames which had been following me all day enveloped the room in a brilliant conflagration, burning my inner world until nothing was left but charcoal and ashes. I surrendered to their hungry touch, allowing the fiery inferno to swallow me whole as I keened until my throat was raw. I grieved until I was empty, oceans of emotion washing out of me and soaking the couch. By the time dawn arrived, I had fallen into an exhausted sleep. Not even the booming bass from the cars of the Crown Vic boys could wake me.

David haunted my dreams that morning and every night after that. Even when my waking mind had moved into the anger and hatred stages of grief several months later, my unconscious mind still sought his embrace. Despite returning to my monk-like devotion to magic, the dreams persisted. I would wake each morning disgusted with myself, angry with my unconscious for betraying me so fully. I knew grief like a best friend. Handling the pain of losing David was a cakewalk in comparison to the black hole I still held within me. Being betrayed by my own brain, however, was something I couldn't handle.

"What's up? Are you ok?" Rhiannon gave me a look that said she knew very well I was not ok, but was giving me the opportunity to confess before she pulled my demons out of me. She knew me well enough to know both when I was upset and when I needed to talk, even if I wasn't willing or ready to admit to either.

"I dreamt about Voldemort again." I grimaced in emphasis, covering my face with my hands.

"I'm gonna go out and have a smoke. Come with?"

I nodded and stood next to my sister as we pulled our shoes from the rack and slid them on before stepping out onto the front porch. I squinted against the bright sunlight, waiting for my eyes and ears to adjust to the change in environment. A gaggle of kids ran past the house into the backyard, laughing and hollering. I smiled at their exuberance, nodding a greeting to their mom and her girlfriend, who sat on their front porch drinking sodas and talking. An older gentleman walked past, his walnut skin glowing golden in the afternoon sun. I took a deep breath and closed my eyes, letting the familiar sounds of the neighbourhood wash over me: neighbours talking, children playing, cars passing, the distant bass of someone's radio pounding. I was home: safe and sound.

"So tell me about this nightmare," Rhiannon said as she pulled a cigarette out and lit it, holding the cylinder between her long, pink fingers.

"It wasn't really a nightmare. In the dream, David and I are still together, but I don't remember how horrible things were. I'm hugging him and loving on him like nothing is wrong. When I wake up, I'm disgusted with myself."

"I think you're still trying to unpack the cognitive dissonance of your breakup. You thought you loved someone and they loved you. Then you woke up from the dream to a harsh reality. Your mind is replaying your breakup."

She had a point. "Yeah, but why? Haven't I suffered enough already? Why is my mind continuing to torture me?"

"Because it doesn't understand yet. How do you feel about the breakup? Do you hate him?"

"No. Confused, I guess. It's like... he's David Tennant and I don't know which is real, the Doctor or Kilgrave."

"When someone shows you who they are..." Rhiannon raised one of her thick walnut eyebrows, prompting me to finish the Maya Angelou quote.

"Believe them."

"Exactly. Who did he show you he was? Who was he on your first date?"

I thought back to our walk in the woods and how he had joked about hiding bodies. I had replied that too many people knew where I was. At the time, I had assumed he was an awkward nerd trying to impress me with his knowledge of forensic science. Now, however, I had more evidence.

"A sociopath."

"Well then, I'd say you already know. But you don't want to admit it. Because you're scared to admit you fell in love with a wannabe serial killer. That wasn't love, honey. That was manipulation. He targeted you." She waved her hand in emphasis, smoke curling upward.

"Yeah, but what if Tom was right?" I shrugged, looking down at the concrete stoop.

"That your superpower is falling for the serial killer in the room?" She took a deep drag off her cigarette and narrowed her hazel eyes.

"Yeah, that. What if I'm cursed? What if I can only love monsters?"

"Because you're secretly a monster?" She raised her eyebrows and stared at me over the rim of her glasses.

"Yes."

Rhiannon threw her head back and exhaled in a sharp, guttural laugh. "You're not a monster. That's some bullshit your parents taught you. And you're not

41

cursed to love serial killers. You were raised by narcissists, so you're easy prey, no offense. What about Raven? Raven isn't a monster. You don't think he would have fallen in love with you if you were one, would he?"

"No. But he's dead."

"Is he?" She put out her cigarette and stood up, staring at me for a moment before turning to go back inside.

I jumped to my feet and followed her. "Wait, what do you mean?"

"Just that. Is he dead? You're the medium. You tell me."

———

I DID NOT IMMEDIATELY RETREAT to the comfort of my long lost love. I was not a damsel in distress. I had studied magic long enough to understand the holographic nature of the universe. Your reality is a reflection of your beliefs and behaviours. I wanted to figure out what I had done wrong. Driven by this — the desire to know — I set out to understand myself.

In magically aware circles, you'll hear many discussions about synchronicity. In a universe of free will, synchronicity is the guiding voice of your Higher Self. Used consistently, synchronicity yields powerful and tangible results. I set my intention for synchronicity to show me what knowledge I needed. The premise was simple. Each morning before getting out of bed, I would set my intention by stating, "I intend to be guided by my Higher Self through synchronicity, intuition, miracles, and other messages so clear they could only have come from me."

I would go about my day maintaining awareness. Awareness is a two-fold process that requires repetition and dedication to develop. The first step is being present. Stop multi-tasking, daydreaming, and worrying. Focus on the task at hand, on your breath, on what it feels like in this moment to be you. When stray thoughts arise, be mindful of them. Be especially alert for sudden bursts of inspiration or spontaneous urges to do activities and follow these. The second step is equanimity and appreciation. Imagine every moment you experience is the "right moment." You are always in the right place at the right time experiencing the right things for your development. Appreciate each moment for its uniqueness and seek the wisdom contained within. Find the beauty in everything; feel gratitude for the profound wonder of being alive.

A wise *sifu* once taught that we are all cups, and only when we are empty, can we learn anything new. In other words, I had to forget what I thought I knew and be receptive and open to new information. Maintaining awareness was a continual subtle adjustment designed to tune the frequency of my etheric body to the vortex; the zero point singularity in which all things existed.

Imagine for a moment your body is a complex scientific instrument capable of returning incredibly detailed information about life, the universe, and your role in it. Your physical body is an earth exploration unit, a vehicle designed to allow you to experience all the myriad wonders of being human and alive. Your vehicle comes equipped with a guidance positioning system intended to assist you in fulfilling your chosen path or destiny in this life. This guidance system is comprised primarily of impulses, emotions, and subtle physical sensations which provide feedback in relation to environmental stimuli.

Modern society and its globalized network of consumerist-driven, materialistic-based logic systems has become so deeply entrenched in the rational part of the human brain that we have all but forgotten the ancient indigenous wisdom of the heart. From birth, we are taught to ignore the subtle messages of our guidance system, convinced by our technological prowess that our emotional and spiritual components are unnecessary. Consequently, in order for our vehicles and their guidance systems to function optimally, a system calibration is required. Our internal systems sometimes require a reset to galactic zero; the open heart of a child.

If I wanted to have a dialogue with the universe, I had to remember how to listen.

5

THE RADIO GODS chose to communicate with me enthusiastically. Beyoncé's throaty voice belted out with strength, transporting me back in time. *"Remember those walls I built, well, baby, they're tumbling down..."*

———

"FOR YOU, MY LOVE." Raven bowed gallantly, producing a small bunch of flowers from behind his back. He held a branch from a hydrangea, one of my favourite flowers because of its propensity for pigment change. The branch was caught mid-state between blue and purple, with ten thousand hues ranging from peri-winkle to lilac to lavender. Through a quirk of nature, this branch had grown into a perfect heart-shaped poof. For a moment, I was speechless. No one had ever brought me flowers before; such romantic things only happened in movies. His gift was more meaningful than movie flowers; the simple perfection of these flowers was far beyond any mass-produced bunch wrapped in cheap cellophane. He had spent time searching for the perfect blossom; I could tell by his pleased expression. He was the embodiment of boyish charm and enthusiasm.

This gesture was more romantic than I deserved. I wasn't the sort of girl who received gifts from suitors. I was the awkward wallflower — curvy musculature too thick for conventional beauty standards — standing along the side-lines trying to fend off the five or six socially inept creepers posing as nice guys while mooning over the homecoming king all night. "Getting the guy" was reserved for those paler skinned, stick-thin beauties whose narrow faces and petite forms conformed to the beauty standards of the dominant culture. Here I was, however, confronted with a scene my rational mind claimed could not exist. A standard issue heartthrob — a guitar-playing, motorcycle-riding, long-haired hunk — was holding flowers. *For me, Miss Awkward Mutt.* He called me his love.

How could this possibly be true? What did he see in me? I tried to imagine the scene from his perspective. I saw a plain, teenage girl, too reminiscent of a Jackson Pollack painting to be pretty, whose clothing was laughably out of fashion — men's skater shoes, worn bell-bottom jeans, and a faded X-Files t-shirt. With her short stature, high cheekbones, and finely sculpted eyebrows, she might have been a China Doll — except for her dark skin and warrior woman physique. Her body — tree-trunk thighs and arms, childbearing hips, generous buttocks and breasts with a tiny muscular waist — might have belonged to a Nubian Queen, except she was too pale. She was always an awkward mutt, stuck between the bloodlines of several peoples, meeting the beauty standards of none.

He was a paragon of diversity: Shunde, Swedish, Irish, and English married into a single sublime specimen, perfect in proportion, his long, rounded nose taking up exactly one third of his face, his cheekbones widening just enough to make him appear sculpted, square chin narrowing beyond the triangular lines of his strong jaw. Full lips accentuated an already expressive bow-shaped mouth. His flawless face had stolen many hearts and inspired more artists than I wanted to think about. How could I compare to any of them? How was I worthy of *him*?

I accepted the bouquet with a gracelessly mumbled thanks, unaware of anything beyond being miserable in my own multi-cultural skin. I only became aware of him again when he stepped into my physical space, gently reaching toward me with outstretched arms. Wordlessly, I stepped into his strong embrace, beleaguered by shame and guilt. He had given me a perfect gift, and I was sulking. *It's a wonder he doesn't give up and leave if this is the way I respond to kindness.* Perhaps a small, dark, secret part of me wanted that to happen. Him breaking my heart would fit perfectly into my tragic sense of self. Unwanted outcasts could have a taste of love — but the illusion should be ripped from them as painfully as possible, proving to them their proper place in the divine cosmic order.

My parents had neither wanted nor loved me. How could anyone else? I genuinely believed I wasn't worth loving; I wasn't pretty, feminine, or normal. In a world of Zeldas and Peaches, I was a Rogue. I was a troubled foster child, an angry, bitter bitch terrified for anyone to touch me lest they reject me for my inhumanity. I was deeply flawed and broken; I sure as hell didn't deserve someone like him. I bit my thick lower lip to keep the tears at bay, promising myself I wouldn't cry. I had always been the ice princess — the defiant, mouthy kid who never let anyone see her weaknesses. I hid my sorrows and my secrets deep inside, keeping everyone around me at arm's length. Despite this, he continually saw through the innumerable walls I built to protect myself; his insight always resulted in an uncomfortable confrontation with my emotions. Secretly, I adored him for it, but I was terrified to admit such a vulnerable truth.

"Want to talk about it?" he asked.

I buried my face in his chest, breathing in the rich earthy smell of him, still trying not to cry. Being in his arms only compounded my misery. I couldn't pretend I wasn't upset if he was going to comfort me as though I clearly was.

"No. Yes. I don't know." I answered as honestly as I could, torn by all the conflicting emotions of adolescence. I longed to let him in. All secrets long to be shared in the light of love. Yet, I yearned to keep my safety too. I excelled in the role of tragic heroine; trauma and misery were my birthright, the fate I felt I deserved. If karma gave out Oscars, I would have already won several for my piteous performances. Romantic lead, I had never studied. I didn't know those lines, or how that story played out; I didn't know what was expected of me. Having typecast myself as the victim for so long, I wasn't entirely certain I trusted this casting not to be a bait and switch.

"What's going on in that beautiful head of yours?" He kissed the top of my head tenderly, his kind words and gentle gesture destroying the last of my hard-won composure.

The dam I had been holding burst at the seams, levees flooded beyond repair. A deluge swept my cheeks, soaking his shirt.

"I'm not beautiful. I don't deserve this." I brandished the heart shaped hydrangea branch. "And I sure as hell don't deserve you." I sniffled.

He pulled me to the couch, sitting so he could hold me and look into my eyes at the same time. "You know, if you spend your whole life comparing yourself to someone else, you will never feel good enough."

He bent his head, looking at me from underneath his dark, heavy eyebrows. Without the charming smile which usually accompanied this look, he was endearingly direct. His expression spoke of painful truth. "Because of who he was, I spent a large portion of my life in my father's shadow. Even if I had grown up to be a dentist, people would still have compared me to him. As his son, there was tremendous pressure and expectation, you know, to be like him. But I'm not him; I'm me. I had to live my own life on my own terms. Only *after* I stopped comparing myself to him was I able to find my own place in life and feel like I was worth something."

He wiped away one of my tears with his thumb. "If you want the hydrangea to be a rose, it seems imperfect and flawed. If you let it be what it is, it's beautiful. I love you — the real you — not the person you pretend to be when everyone else is looking. Not because of who you aren't, but because of who you are. The things you consider flaws are the things which made me fall in love with you. I think the day you let yourself be the person you are, you'll be able to see what I see. I only wish I could show it to you."

———

MY THOUGHTS RETURNED to the present. Beyoncé was still singing. I was crying.

"Hit me like a ray of sun, burning through my darkest night…"

I caught a glimpse of my reflection in the window, the darkened sky beyond the glass turning the surface into a mirror. I suddenly felt all the more *verklempt* — overwhelmed by joyful tears. Indescribable surges of love and gratitude washed over me in overwhelming waves, causing hot saline to cascade down my cheeks in waterfalls of worship. Inexplicably, I recognized the woman I saw there. The graceful sweep of her magenta-purple ombré curls as they fell about her shoulders, the youthful appearance which belied her age. I saw the secret smile struggling to break the clouds of tears, the high cheekbones and dimples, the perfectly-arched eyebrows. The uneven melanin I had once hated now made my skin seem star-studded. She was beautiful, powerful, and strong. He had been right, all those years ago. I had always been beautiful, but only when I stopped trying to be like everyone else did I shine. My heart overflowed with newfound appreciation for him. In a world where lovers tried to change each other, he had always held space for me to be myself, waiting for me to realize the truth he had already seen.

6

THE DIFFICULTY with a love affair which had never been based in the physical was its ephemeral, evanescent nature. In the physical realm, couples maintain and renew their emotional connection in a variety of ways. Spending time together, of course, is the easiest and most accessible method. Those in long distance relationships must resort to other means: letters, phone calls, video chats, occasional visits. When the person you love is separated from you by time and space and there is no phone call to connect you, maintaining the awareness of your connection is more challenging, especially when you are alone in the knowledge of your love. Consider this: mated couples frequently pair up in friend groups where members swap stories about their respective partners in acts of bonding. In doing so, their minds are focused on their love and their memories validated by the group consciousness. Remembering your love through storytelling inspires the brain to produce the neurochemicals of love: oxytocin, dopamine, and serotonin.

As Rhiannon was the only one who had ever met him, I had none other than my sister with whom I could share my memories. Privacy was rare and we were both scared of being considered crazy so we didn't often have opportunities to discuss my relationship with Raven. As far as the muggles who made up the majority of the world would believe, my love was an illusion. I lacked the toolset to effectively maintain the hormones of love. Consequently, my awareness of him faded. Memories were powerful motivators, but they were only memories. As much as I may have felt surrounded by his embrace, my sense of connection had a temporary half-life, beyond which it was doomed to decay.

When I was younger, the euphoric decline would result in my inexorable collapse into a tenebrous depression. As much as I longed for his light, the absence of it was too painful. I no longer slid into the abyss of self-harm, but only because I would not allow myself. Years of dogged persistence in the art of self-preservation had long ago created neural pathways for denial. I was a master of the disassociation government agencies would have loved to exploit for their own gains; entire years of my childhood were blank nothings. With the practiced manner of a seasoned veteran, my rational mind would slip into my conscious mind like a triage unit, pulling my awareness out of the dangers of the combat zone. For reasons I did not then understand, I would forget, slipping away into the safety of my daily routine.

The universe is a persistent partner, willing to wait out my denial. I kept setting an intention to be guided, and the universe kept responding.

It was game night, and we — my close-knit group of friends and I — had gathered for our regular role-playing game. As the Storyteller for this chronicle, I sat at the head of the table, a black three-ring binder containing all my notes at the ready, my piles of ten-sided dice separated by colour — clear, green, and pastels. You can't use the same dice for NPCs and villains; it just isn't right. As my players stood up to leave the table for their "corporate smoke break," I wondered at the joy of being with all of them: the eldest of my younger brothers, my sister, and our whole extended family of misfit friends. I was blessed with a sense of completion when we were all together like this. A thread of their conversation stole through the window and into my conscious. Unexpectedly, I slipped off into the past.

———

I LAY with my head on Raven's shoulder, looking up at the night sky. The evening had been perfectly lovely, but I still couldn't shake the sense of melancholy filling the air. A shooting star shot across the sky and I found myself immersed in a memory I had lost to time.

· · ·

THE ANIMALS FED and put away for the night, I trudged toward the makeshift gate, milk pan in hand. A shooting star streaked across the sky, drawing my attention up. I was suddenly and inexplicably filled with a deep sense of longing and homesickness. I knew instinctively — in the way children know —the people I missed so desperately were light years away. I also knew I would be missing them for a long time. I have no idea how long I stood there, crying up at the night sky, begging to go home.

❀ ❀ ❀

The depth of my ancient *hiraeth* washed over me anew and hot tears seeped out of my eyes. I blinked quickly, trying to keep them away from his shoulder. I didn't want to spoil our date. He knew, as always.

"Kara? What's wrong, my love?" he asked, reaching to wipe my tears away with his thumb.

I shook my head in response, beginning to truly cry. A torrent of tears washed down my cheeks. I shook silently. He rolled over, wrapping his arms around me and kissing the top of my head. I wasn't ready to talk about it yet. He rested his sculpted cheek on my head and rubbed my back in slow strokes. I could feel him pulling the sorrow down through my channels so that it passed out of me and I began to relax. We lay there for a seeming eternity; time lost all meaning. He was patient and content, waiting for me to be ready to speak.

"It's stupid. Nothing important," I muttered into his muscular chest.

He laughed and stroked my long cranberry hair.

"Everything you think and feel is important to me. Intelligent as you are, I highly doubt it will be stupid. Try me." He somehow managed to make vulnerable moments of intimacy feel like truth or dare, more thrilling than terrifying. As a tactic, it often produced fantastic results. I loved that about him. Or I would, after I had confessed.

"It's crazy. You wouldn't understand."

He laughed again, using one calloused hand to gently tilt my cleft chin so I was looking up at him. As much as I wanted to resist, his tender gaze melted through the frozen walls of my fear. "You're dating a dead man. Crazy went out the window a while ago. Try me. You might be surprised what I have the capacity to understand."

"I miss them." I mumbled, reluctant to speak my truth.

"Who?" He asked, his voice soft and gentle.

"I don't know." I shook my head, trying to avoid eye contact. Our position made doing so all but impossible. "When I look at the stars, it reminds me of them. I don't know if I'll ever see them again."

He smiled and kissed my crown. "We have all lived and loved many times. It's natural to create bonds of destiny which tie us to other lives. It's natural to miss them. Don't worry, love. Fate brought us together even though I was already dead. Those others you miss, you will find them too."

"How do you know?"

"I just do. Such is the way of life. The longing you feel is the pull of fate."

I thought for a moment, staring up into his warm hazel eyes. As profound as this conversation might be, my raging hormones reminded me he was holding me incredibly close. I tried not to be aware of all the places our bodies touched, or the incredibly electric heat generated at those points of contact. "So, you're saying this is destiny?"

"Definitely."

❊ ❊ ❊

My mind connects ideas based on subject matter. Moments separated by time become linked in the holistic organization system of my memory banks. Another memory I had forgotten followed the first in short succession; links in the long, winding chains of recollection. I was once more engulfed in my past; lost to the present in the spontaneous magic of memory.

"WHAT'S ON YOUR MIND, my love?" He wore his all-knowing smirk.

I was well acquainted with this look, as he wore it often. One corner of his bow-shaped mouth quirked up, an eyebrow raised, and tell-tale creases appeared at the corners of his hazel eyes. He would tilt his head and smile enigmatically from underneath his full eyebrows. The look was one part smart-ass, two parts coy, boyish charm. Such a look usually meant I was about to learn about myself.

"Do you miss them?" I began twisting a corner of

my plaid grey flannel shirt around in my hands. Doing so gave me an excuse to break eye contact. If I didn't look at him, he might not notice the moisture in the corner of my eyes or all the unanswered questions underneath the surface. He might not realize the question was about me. I knew my misdirection was pure foolishness. His insight and awareness were the loadstone that had drawn my heavy-leaded self to him. He would see all the things I tried so valiantly to conceal. I had to pretend I could hide from him, however. I had my dignity to preserve.

"Miss who?" *Fair enough.* I was pretending. He was playing along. *Bless his heart.*

"Your family." I twisted the shirt tighter, until the fabric made quiet creaking noises in my hands. I was still avoiding the real question. "Her."

"Ahh," he sighed, knowingly. I could hear him moving closer. This conversation was going to involve eye contact and emotional intimacy. I twisted the shirt even tighter. *Why did I have to ask such things? What was wrong with me?* "Kara," he began, not quite a question, but a request. I knew he would wait to speak until I looked at him. As much as I wanted him to lift my chin up and force me to look at him, he wouldn't. We would sit here all afternoon waiting if that's what I required to relent. Damn his Aquarian patience! I sighed and met his eyes reluctantly.

"You deserve an answer. But there isn't an answer to give that won't hurt you. If I tell you my life with her meant nothing to me, I would be lying. More than that, such a statement would be disloyal. Having said such, how could you ever trust me? If I could betray her so easily, what about you? And yet, if I tell you I love her, how can you trust me?" His eyes widened slightly and he frowned. We sat there for a heartbeat, maybe more. It was my turn to be patient.

He sighed. "Yes, I miss her. Yes, I still love her."

I was going to twist this shirt into ribbons. My hands had begun to cramp and turn colours, but the fabric wasn't broken yet. Only a single red thread had escaped. I couldn't bear to meet his eyes. Strong, slim fingers appeared in my vision, a gesture of invitation, no more. I released the shirt, my fingers briefly locked in tension. Shakily, I laid my hand in his. My hands were so small in comparison; broad palms with short, stocky fingers in sharp contrast to his long, graceful digits. *How can we possibly be a good match for each other?* He was beautiful: strong, dexterous, funny. I was not. Focusing on our hands protected me from having to see that the pain on his face mirrored my own. A single teardrop splashed into our hands. *His? Or my own?*

We were both crying when I looked up.

"Have you ever tried to... talk to her?" In asking him impossible questions which would only hurt us both, I was hitting the bullseye with record breaking precision. I couldn't stop asking them, however. I had to know.

"Yes." His eyes darkened and his features drew in. He was a thundercloud, dark and filled with repressed emotions. His shoulders were tense, pulled closer to his ears than could be comfortable. When he spoke again, his voice was quiet, shaken. "Right after it happened, I spent days trying to talk to her. I screamed. I begged. I cried. I even went to my funeral. But she couldn't hear me. And I couldn't bear to watch her grieve, knowing I was unable to comfort her. Finally, I stopped. It wasn't helping either of us move on."

"What inspired you to stop?" *Was I trying to torture him or myself?* But I had to know. As he had said, his past actions had relevance. As he had treated her, he would likely treat me.

He laughed, short and abruptly, without mirth. "My dad."

"Your dad?"

"He died when I was so young, you know? So, when I saw him standing there holding out his hand, I took it, without any conscious thought. I was a child again, and here was my dad, coming to make me feel safe. Of course I went with him." As he spoke of his father, his sculpted face softened. For a moment, I could see the lost little boy he kept hidden from the world. This only made me love him more.

"What about the rest of your family?"

"My mother was heartbroken. It's not easy to lose a child, you know. Especially after losing my dad. I wasn't there to make her laugh anymore." The lost little boy resurfaced.

"And your sister?" My voice broke this time. *Finally, the real question.*

"Every day. For a while, I followed her everywhere trying to protect her. But she's too sensitive; she could feel me with her. At some point, I realized she wasn't going to be able to grieve with me there, you know?"

He swallowed thickly, tears streaming down his oblong face. "I still check in on her."

I couldn't see him anymore; the torrent of tears rendered him a blurry mirage. I became aware I was shaking, quiet sobs escaping in gasping breaths. He opened his arms and I crawled into them, surrendering to emotion. Time stretched into an endless infinity as we sat there — the gravity of our love distorting the fabric of space-time — sobbing onto each other's shoulders. By the end, our shirts were sopping wet and our faces were red, puffy messes.

Love is ugly crying together over familiar pain and finding comfort in raw intimacy. Love is the safety of sharing our suffering as deeply and freely as our joy.

"Your brothers?"

I nodded, teary-eyed, and swallowed hard. "I'm not there to protect them anymore. They have new, *'forever'* families now."

I could see in his eyes he understood. He pulled me closer into a strong embrace. I imagined I could hear his heartbeat. "You'll see them again."

"How do you know?" My voice was muffled by the folds of his cotton shirt. Was this his uncanny prescience again?

"I just do." He kissed the top of my head. For the moment, his certainty was enough.

———

I RETURNED to the present with a newfound awareness and appreciation for the strings of fate. My life had been shaped by the ever-present ache of longing; the heartache of missing those I loved. My sense of loss and longing had been an inescapable misery, an event horizon so large no light ever escaped. Over time, the pain faded as I found them. In the precision of hindsight, the contrast was staggering: a blinding light after an eternity of darkness. For a certainty, I would meet others along the way with whom instant recognition and easy rapport would develop into lifelong friendship. For now, knowing I was surrounded by those I missed before I knew them was an emotional revelation of truth. The faces of those I had found since the shooting stars filled my mind: my adoptive sister, Rhiannon; my starbother, Thor; my soul-sister Cobra Lay-dee. My brothers had also returned to my life as predicted. He had always known. My heart spasmed in gratitude, releasing waves of relief and love.

From that beautiful moment of realization my heart made a quantum leap which left my brain gasping. *If they could find their way into my life, why not him? Could it be possible?* It had been so long since I had dared to hope. The memories which insisted upon returning to me pulled at my heart and soul with the inevitable arms of gravity. They would not be denied.

Neither would my survival instincts. The triage unit entered while I slept, slipping away with my realization and placing it far from the light of day. Such was my cycle. Synchronistic message of hope was inevitably followed by fearful response from rational mind. Conscious "me" would forget. Intention to receive synchronicity would provoke reasonable response from the Universe. You can't simultaneously chase your destiny while also hiding from it. I was a hamster stuck in a cosmic wheel, spinning around and around in the gravitational well spun from my own denial. The cycle was dizzying.

7

I walked into the empty bathroom, the sharp staccato of my heels echoing off the cement walls seeming unnaturally loud in the industrial space. This bathroom had always slightly unnerved me as a child. To be honest, the whole basement had. Basements always managed to be creepy, especially ones attached to haunted old buildings. Of course, as a child, I had never spent any time down here after dark either. I had always gone home when the library closed at five. Only the truly mad or desperate would have tried to stay hidden here at night.

Intellectually, I knew there were thirty other people in the building, far more than I had ever been here with. Technically, I was far from alone. On the other hand, they were all two floors above me, and none of them — save Rhiannon — could have helped me much anyway. I consciously pushed away those old memories, focusing instead on my reflection in the mirror, wiping away small smudges of mascara and eyeliner. My crying-with-mascara-on skills did not extend to all-natural mineral makeup, nor to the volume of tears I had shed.

Part of me felt neurotic about having cried in front of so many of my family and friends. The rest of me tried to shrug it off as normal. People cry at weddings. They normally don't cry when they're the ones offici-ating the wedding, but how could I not have cried? In the moment, saying the ceremonial words Rhiannon had prepared, I had been overwhelmed by the love I felt in the room. To be fair, most of the attendees had been crying too.

I was so intent on checking my makeup and reas-suring myself that I hadn't felt or heard the presence of the ghost before she arrived. Instead, I looked up from the sink to see her reflection in the mirror behind me. I jumped, grabbing the sink for support as I came back down on the short heels I had chosen to wear. The ghost giggled, covering her mouth and shaking her head; her birch-coloured pageboy bobbed up and down with the motion. She was still as playful as always.

"Hi." I smiled at her in the mirror and turned around to face her, being careful not to lean up against the sink. I didn't want to have a wet butt when I went back upstairs.

"I know you, but you got old." She cocked her head to the side, regarding me with a seriousness that seemed at odds with her young age.

I tried not to be wounded by her innocent words. She was an ageless child and would stay young forever unless she crossed over. She had played with me when we were the same age. Seeing me as an adult now had to be jarring. Still, my ego stung. I had inherited my birth family's ageless complexion and was often mistaken for a teenager. Leave it to a ghost to call me old. Not even the kids in my family would do that.

"Yeah." I agreed noncommittally, biting back my smart comment. *People do that.* She was a kid. She didn't deserve my sarcasm. It wasn't her fault she was dead. She had to be lonely. "I remember you too. Thank you." She was the little girl who had saved me from the scarier ghosts who roamed these halls. She had made it safe for me to use the bathroom in peace as a sensitive child.

She smiled awkwardly and ducked her head. I'm sure she would have blushed if she had been alive. "It was nothing. Momma always said if you could do a kindness for somebody you ought to because it was the proper Christian thing to do."

The bleak sadness in her voice was heart-breaking. I wondered why she had been trapped here for so long. Surely her mother had died long ago. "You must miss her, sweetie. Would you like to see her again?"

"I would, but she told me to wait here for her. She said she'd be by to pick me up from school and not to leave or she'd have to use the switch."

My heart spasmed in sympathy. No wonder she was still here. "Well, I just saw her upstairs looking for you. Would you like me to take you to her?"

"Please?" I could tell she was trying not to cry.

I smiled at her gently and reached toward her. "C'mon, sweetie. Let's go find your mom."

I felt a tingle where she placed her small hand in mine and swallowed back tears. I had to fake a smile for her. I was the adult now. I could protect her. As we climbed the ancient wooden stairs together, I shifted my awareness to the double doors at the front of the building, opening a portal to the other side. I prayed her mother would in fact be waiting and come to collect her, just as she had promised.

She must have. When we reached the doors, my small companion let go of my hand and broke into a run, grinning from ear to ear at something only she could see. She paused on the threshold and turned back momentarily to wave at me.

"Thank you."

"It was nothing. It was the proper thing to do. Say hi to your mother for me."

She smiled and turned back, disappearing through the doors. I closed the gateway and headed back upstairs to the wedding.

My niece met me at the door to the stairway, grabbing my hand and pulling me after her. "C'mon, Aunt Kara. It's time for food and then cake and then dancing!"

I laughed at her exuberance and squeezed her hand, feeling protective and sentimental after my encounter below. She was much younger than my ghostly friend, and I found myself praying she would continue to age. I pushed the morbid thoughts away, reminding myself I was here to celebrate.

Laureen slipped her hand from mine and dashed into the room, running back to the table nearby where she sat with her parents. I wished I had been seated with them as I was intended to be. Instead I was at the table of last-minute additions. While we had been taking family photos, the guests had seated themselves, overriding Rhiannon's seating arrangement. I got it. I just didn't like it. Laureen's father passed me on his way to the buffet table, his smile genial.

"You're next," he said quietly with a playful wink and a half-hug before grabbing a plate.

If only. Oh, how I wished that were true. Sitting alone at my sister's wedding — the last single one in our group — I felt Raven's absence more keenly than ever. Weddings were always hard, but this one was particularly so. Seeing how happy my family was for Rhiannon — seeing how happy she and Bevan were together — made me even more aware of what I was missing. All I had ever wanted was the simple blessing of pledging my love in front of my family and friends. After all, everyone else in my friend circle had that. Except for me.

At the next table, Laureen and her little brother A.T. were giggling at something, their dark heads drawn together in laughter. I sighed quietly, my stomach sinking even lower. Not only was I the last one to be married, I would be the last one to have kids. Melissa already had two. Rhiannon's first was secretly already underway. Mine did not yet exist, except as ephemeral figments of my longing and imagination.

I wanted to watch my grandmother read my children stories, to see them climb up in her lap and cover her in sticky kisses. I ached to hold their heavy bodies in my arms as they slept, to watch their father play with them, to see him carry them tenderly in his arms, to witness the beauty of his love for them as he showered them with affection. I longed to watch my children play together with their cousins, to swap parenting advice and knowing smiles with the others of my generation. I wanted to belong, to be part of the family in a contributing way. Instead, I was forever on the outside, stuck at the singles' table, eating my veggie pizza and trying, once again, not to cry.

All too soon, it was time to cut the cake. I joined the rest of the guests as we clustered around the cake table. Flashes fired as people took photographs around me. I tried to focus on how happy my sister looked, how deeply she was smiling. For the most part, I managed, at least until it was time for them to eat the cake. She and Bevan faced each other and I saw his face light up with a mischievous grin. Rhiannon narrowed her eyes at him playfully, warning him not to act on the impish impulse he was telegraphing.

I swallowed back a lump of sorrow, recognizing the wordless way they were able to communicate. I could too easily imagine the same playful look on Raven's face and knew my response would not be entirely different from my sister's. I consciously pushed away the fantasy with a pang of guilt. This was my sister's day. I should be happy for her, not feeling sorry for myself. Try as I might, I couldn't quite shake the melancholy ache suffusing my being. Not even my favourite gluten-free vegan carrot cake helped.

Dancing made things easier, at least at first. Being

a revolving dance partner for the children was a blast. They didn't mind when I slipped off my shoes and spun in silly circles with them. A.T. and I swept across the floor with him on my hips, pretending to ballroom dance. All too soon they tired and sat down, leaving me on my own just as the slow dancing began. Rhiannon and Bevan took to the dance floor along with the other couples, staring lovingly into each other's eyes.

I stared at the floor, thinking of Raven, wishing he were here to dance with me. As much as I endeavoured not to miss him, milestone moments such as these made such a task Herculean. On any given day, the hole in my life was a dull ache, the quiet roar of the ocean waves, a missing limb whose phantom pain was so familiar I could almost forget the torment because I wasn't looking directly at the stump. Sitting here, witnessing their love, I might as well have been a paraplegic at a tap-dancing contest, painfully aware of all I had lost and was missing.

Seeing everyone I love celebrate the romance in their lives was a bittersweet reminder of the hidden agony I still bore. They had no way of knowing my heart was an open wound; their happily-ever-afters were fresh salt mixed with a gallon of rubbing alcohol and topped with a dash of capsaicin for good measure. The black hole was heavier than lead, sinking through my stomach and pinning me to the floor. I focused on the grooves and whirls of the old woodgrain, blinking away tears. I did *not* want to go back down to the basement to check my makeup again.

Alicia Keys' voice broke into my reverie, drawing me back into the past.

"Some people want it all, but I don't want nothing at all, if it ain't you baby, if I ain't got you baby..."

———

THE SMELL of jasmine incense filled the air, and candles lent the room a golden glow. A radio played a love ballad quietly in the background, a man's voice rising and falling with emotion. I sat on a bean bag chair, twisting the edge of my t-shirt in my hands, trying desperately not to cry. His graceful hands slipped into my field of vision, obscuring the shirt.

"May I?" he asked.

I placed my hands in his, allowing him to pull me to my feet. When he wore his mischievously charming smile, resistance was impossible. I smiled back despite myself. He led me around the small room in a silly spinning dance, more playful than romantic. Soon, we were laughing and twirling like children. Eventually, we collapsed on the floor in a fit of giggles, dizzy and punch drunk with glee. We lay there together, catching our breath and staring at the ceiling.

"Want to talk about it yet?" He rolled toward me, one eyebrow raised and a hint of a smile playing at the corner of his mouth. I found his smile the most irresistible trait he possessed and he knew it.

"Prom," I sighed.

"I thought conversation involved more than monosyllabic responses, my love."

I growled. "What is there to explain? It's exactly like every other 'magical coming of age moment' in my life. Fucking ruined." My tone could have melted metal.

I sat up forcefully, needing to shout at the fucking ceiling. "What the fuck did I ever do to you, Gods? Why do you put me through this shit?!" Hot, angry tears streamed down my face as I turned to him. "You wouldn't understand. You *got* to have a life. You were happy when you died. Being with you is the closest I've ever come to happy. It's a cruel joke. Because I'll never get to go to prom with you, or marry you, or have babies with you, or any of the other *normal* things I wanted for my life." The long-smouldering coals of resentment caught fire inside my soul.

I wanted the words back in my mouth as badly as I wanted to have said them. The flicker of pain across his face was sickeningly satisfying and heart-breaking at the same time. He was always so calm and happy, like everything in life (and death, apparently) was a joke to him. As much as I loved him for this peculiar equanimity, I also wanted to hate him a little, too. If he truly loved me, why wasn't he suffering as I was? Finally given the space to breathe, the flames in my heart intensified.

"My whole life, I've always been the good girl, the 'chosen one.' Teacher's Pet. Honour Roll. Academically Gifted. I went to church every Sunday and most Wednesdays too, when I was old enough. I paid my tithe. I got up in the middle of the night to feed babies and change diapers. I got up at four in the morning to milk goats and feed rabbits. I collected eggs. I said my prayers and read my scriptures, multiple times. And for what?!" I sucked in a deep breath, feeling the conflagration in my core growing into an explosive inferno. My face was flushed with anger I had held inside for too long. "For the state to come and take it all away in a heartbeat. For everything to turn out to be a big fat lie. *Family is forever. The church is your family. You're God's chosen.*" My voice dripped with derision and mockery.

"And where are they now? Gone! My life is nothing but ashes. I've lost my entire world. No matter what, my old life is never coming back."

At some point in my fiery tirade, I had risen to my feet in anger. I found myself looking down at him, sobbing. "You are the best thing in my life, and you are not alive. I've given up so many dreams: being an astronaut, or a fighter pilot, going into space. I wanted to be a normal sixteen-year-old girl for once, going to prom with the boy she loves." Emotionally spent, I stared blankly at him while my chest heaved, rising and falling at an erratic *prentissimo* pace.

With a dragon's grace, he rose to his feet in a serpentine movement. "I'm sorry." He opened his arms in a gesture of invitation and welcome. I stepped into them and practically fell against his chest, still crying. "Do you want me to leave?" His voice was quiet, melancholy.

"No," I sobbed harder, clinging to his shirt.

The song on the radio changed; another gentle R&B song wafted out. This time it was the harmonic crooning of All 4 One.

"I can love you like that. I would make you my world; move Heaven and Earth, if you were my girl..."

He began to sway with me gently.

"I may not be able to go to your prom with you, but I can dance with you. As I remember, that's the important part about prom." He led me in a slow, swirling dance.

I closed my eyes, resting my head against his shoulder, letting him guide our etheric bodies around the room in an effortless dance. I lost myself in the sensation of his shoulder underneath my cheek, the weight of his arms around my waist, the serpentine dragon's grace he possessed. I memorized the way he smelled, clean and crisp, like a forest after the rain.

Either one of us could have, at any point, rearranged the astral place in which we danced to resemble my prom. Streamers, balloons, people... anything we imagined would have been possible had we chosen to concentrate. We could have changed our appearances, donning formal attire. We could have been our own fairy godmothers and spun up a night to remember for all time. He was right, though; we didn't need to. I didn't care about prom. I cared about dancing with him. I would remember this moment forever, without any of the culturally-expected pomp.

We danced all night in his shabby chic "living" space, in worn shirts and jeans, barefoot.

8

SOME DAYS WERE BETTER than others. Some mornings, I would awaken fresh from the Dreamscape, caught in the trap of terror. Often, the terror was caused by a nightmare about the ex; his casual callousness and complete disregard for my emotions replayed in painful scenario after painful scenario. Other times, the nightmare was an autocratic government bent on absolute control whose forces I and those I protected were forced to flee. Tyranny and trauma had been the themes of my childhood and often reared their ugly heads with timeless precision. The uncomfortable cognitive dissonance of hope spurred my mind to retreat into the comfortable known of despair.

Sometimes, this horror-filled headspace lasted for days or weeks. Once, the headspace persisted for an entire month. No matter how familiar a face depression was for me, I did not welcome it. Doggedly, I persisted. I carved out time each morning for my own healing space, spending an hour or two dedicated to my practice. Practice often seemed a Sisyphean effort, where I gained ground only to slip to the bottom of my hamster wheel, exhausted. Despite this trend, I stubbornly persisted.

Without my notice, I began to change. For most of my life, I had most decidedly *not* been a morning person. I would awaken angry at the world, full of angst and fear. I would have found a flaw to complain about: the glass I wanted to use was not clean, I burned my breakfast, and someone had drunk all the tea. Now, I began to be pleasant. I woke with a smile, and although I was perhaps not the happiest camper in the campground, I was at least capable of being nice to others. The tightness in my chest began to fade with the tension in my shoulders, followed by the cramps in my stomach. I began to experience intermittent periods of peace, during which I would marvel at the dissolution of my stress.

The messages from the universe persisted. This time, the cosmos chose a child for its mouthpiece. I sat on the edge of a cement planter, keeping an eye on two teenagers goofing off nearby. Technically, their nanny should have been doing this, but she was flustered this morning. We all were. Navigating a fourteen-footer through downtown Atlanta after five days of minimal sleep and even less food challenged everyone's patience. Add in the special needs of adults with health challenges and neuro-divergent genius children who had been away from their comfort zone too long and tempers would inevitably rise. As the adult least flus-

78

tered and most likely to get along with the kids this early in the morning, I volunteered to watch them. I found their youthful exuberance easier to handle than the adults and their jangled nerves.

The brothers chased each other around the small patio, one in sneakers and the other on wheels. Their laughter echoed off the textured cement around me, distracting me from the ever-present din of traffic and people. I smiled as I watched them, enjoying their enthusiasm. Seeing her brothers were already occupied and would not compete for my attention, Cassie seized the opportunity, bounding toward me with a wide grin overtaking her narrow, elfin face. In the time-honoured tradition of pre-teenage pubescent girls, she had imprinted upon me as her femmespiration. I was doing my best not to disappoint her.

"You're so pretty," she said, smiling up at me and squinting against the sunlight peaking over the edges of the buildings.

"Thank you, sweetie. You are too, you know." I returned her smile, putting as much love into the gesture as I could. If showering her with affection could do anything to ease the wounds to her fragile self-esteem caused by bullying, I would gladly give her endless praise.

"Are you married?" She twirled a strand of honey-coloured hair around her finger.

I felt as though she had punched me. Not deliberately of course, but there is always that moment in childhood awkwardness when a growing body with unknown strength escapes the young mind controlling it to injure the adult they are playing with. So too with words. Children's insight can be just as unintentionally wounding.

"Um..." I faltered, torn between my evolutionary mammalian instinct to protect the youngling at any cost and my own need for privacy. "Yes and no."

"Are you divorced?" She squinted even further, wrinkling her fawn forehead.

"No." My answer sounded harsher than I had intended, and I sought to correct it. "I was never legally married. But I was handfasted. It's kind of like a wedding, the old-fashioned kind our ancestors used to do. Your mom and dad were handfasted too, you know." I hoped to distract her by mentioning her parents. Most children are eager to learn family secrets, and I gambled she would be too.

"But mom and dad got legally married too. Why didn't you?" She leaned closer. Nope, not this kid. She was too smart for me.

"I was a teenager. I wasn't old enough to be legally married." *Ok, so maybe not entirely the truth. But what am I supposed to say? He was dead? Her parents would definitely thank me for that one.*

"Ooh." She nodded her pointy chin slowly, her bob bouncing with the motion. "Why didn't you get married when you grew up?"

Ouch, kid. Her baby giraffe kicks felt aimed with divine precision.

"We lost touch with each other. His parents took him to China. I was in foster-care and got moved to another placement." *Another faerie lie, though technically true. What exactly should I say? He's dead, Jim?*

"Death cannot stop true love. True love comes back." She nodded with the innocent certainty of a child, her eyebrows narrowing in an earnest expression of deep-seated conviction. *And I thought I was the mentor here.* Her expression quickly turned into a smile, and she threw herself at me in a quick hug before scampering away to chase her brothers. I sat there, stunned at the turn in our conversation almost as much as I was by the hug.

Fortunately for me, there was a five-plus-hour ride home during which to consider her wisdom. Somewhere in Northern Georgia, the weekend of constant socialization wore upon all our minds and conversations lapsed in favour of the radio and retreat into our own respective worlds. The rocking motion of the truck pulled me into a semi-trance state. Drawn in by the powerful lure of remembrance sparked by Cassie's words, I surrendered to the strong current of recall and sank beneath its anachronistic waves.

———

BEING BLINDFOLDED HEIGHTENED my other senses. Movements in the air currents, smells, and sounds all deepened in sensation as I was forced to focus on them. Temporarily lacking eyesight also heightened awareness of my auric body. If I focused on the energy currents around me, I could sense where things were, especially people. Being blindfolded also intensified my awareness of emotions. I was intimately aware of how close Raven stood to me, the places where our etheric fields overlapped. His excitement washed over me as he checked the blindfold to be certain it was comfortable. His enthusiasm was infectious. Endemic excitement was an entirely new experience for me.

Unaware, I had spent my entire life in a state of constant, quiet panic. I slept slightly, alert to any sound. Once, my sister took a photo of me literally sleeping with one of my eyes half-opened. I faced the door whenever possible, preferring a line of sight which allowed me to observe each person who entered a room and gauge their threat level. I often listened and energetically "felt" for people behind me, ensuring no-one could ever sneak up on me. I apologized constantly, assuming everything my fault. I was perpetually waiting to be yelled at, alert for the slap I hadn't seen coming. Sometimes, I waited for the switch, the flyswatter, or the belt. I had been raised by two damaged fire signs. They lived by the old adage about rods and spoiling children. I hadn't been spoiled, at all.

In any other circumstance, this space would have terrified me and reduced me to the survival instincts of a caged animal; in this circumstance, the space became a powerful place to observe. The initial panicked cramps of my stomach had been gently dissuaded by my attention and awareness. *Hush*, I said to myself. *I trust him.* For his part, his mirthful smile and barely contained gaiety continued to be highly effective. His natural ability to be cheerfully contagious was the catalyst I needed to allow myself fresh perspective. In my experience, people preparing to hurt you telegraphed their intention through physical gestures, facial expressions, and (most tellingly) their emotions. Raven's innocent exuberance had all the guile of a puppy at a play. I instinctively knew whatever surprise lay ahead of me was a joyful one. As a result, I felt empowered to enjoy his surprise and determinedly focused my efforts on doing so.

Satisfied I was comfortable and unable to see, he gently took my hand, leading me. I stumbled several times; each time, he gently supported and stabilized me until I found my balance again. Each time I stumbled, the space I would have normally filled with deprecation for my clumsiness was filled instead with good-natured laughter. "Whoops," he would say, with a laugh, which rippled out into my energy, catching me as effectively as a giggle ball. Soon, we were chortling like a pair of giddy children.

Our excursion may have taken mere minutes, or hours. With him, moments such as these were timeless; he had the power to still the universe into pausing for an eternity, the gravitational pull of our love stretching the fabric of space-time into an endless infinity. This peculiar magic of his was a side effect of the mindful way he approached life, with genuine appreciation for every single, messy moment. The true magic of living in the now is the powerful ability to transcend time itself.

A lifetime of laughter later, my sides aching, we stopped in an unknown somewhere. There was a pressure in the air, ripples of excited expectation brushed against my skin in the flutter of ten thousand butterfly wings. I could hear quiet music drifting from some-where. Etta James's powerful voice floated from the edges, a timeless postcard from the past. Raised as I was in an anachronistic childhood of TV-Land and war-era classics, the music was comfortable. I had danced to this song so many times, happily imagining love with the puritanical innocence of pre-war Americana. The synchronicity of his musical selection made my heart swell with love. The subtle scent of jasmine hovered in the air, with a hint of honeysuckle and roses, as though we stood in a garden. I was aware of the ebb and flow of energy around us, the echoes of living things. *Definitely a garden*, I thought.

The awareness of him turning to face me was intense. He raised his arms around me to untie the blindfold, his familiar wood scent washing over me in waves. He lifted the fabric from my eyes with gentle hands, and I was dizzy and dazzled by the lights for a moment. Tiny twinkling strands of bulbs hung between the most beautiful trees I had ever seen. Fragrant flowers, white roses and night-blooming jasmine, rioted around us in efflorescent abandon. Fireflies danced beyond the edges of the clearing. The tableau before me looked so much like the Faerie of my childhood. I was swept away by emotion, soaring down a river of love. Teary-eyed and beaming, I committed each magical detail to memory. He stood nearby, watching me, his smile growing in tandem with mine.

I turned my attention to him. *Where are we? What is he up to?* "What is all of this?"

"A surprise." He threw his arms wide open in a

charmingly dramatic gesture, grinning from ear to ear. "Do you like it?" His boyish vulnerability was peeking through again.

"I love it." I wrapped my arms around him in a quick, spontaneous hug before pulling back to look up into his eyes. "But... what is it?"

He laughed, throwing his head back with abandon before fixing me with his playful smile. "Come on, I'll show you." I took the hand he offered, willing to follow his eager lead. He reminded me of an exuberant puppy, and I loved him all the more for the resemblance. Excitement wasn't an emotion I had ever learned. Experiencing enthusiasm vicariously through him was the ecstatic realization of spiritual truth. I hadn't known anyone could be happy in such a manner.

He raised an arm, deftly brushing aside a living curtain of foliage and flowers. I admired the effortless grace of his movements, the way he lived in a perpetual state of water-like flow. We entered a small space under the branches of a tree, a room created by nature. Through the curtain of branches, I could see the lights of the larger garden twinkling with the magic of hope. Our sheltered space was lit by a single candle, set on a table standing at the base of the tree. The altar held a silver dish, a red cord, a goblet, a ring, and a knife. I began to cry, quietly.

Raven turned to look at me, concern flashing across his features. "Love?" He sounded uncertain.

Unable to articulate, I looked deep into his eyes, pouring my emotion through my own; praying it was possible to reverse the polarity of my empathy. I placed my hand over his heart, imagining my palms were tiny vortices of energy like an anime monk.

"Thank you." I hoped my simple words were enough. They didn't feel like enough to me. Someone had finally seen me — for exactly who I was — and offered love unflinching. *How could I put such a feeling into words in a way he would understand?* For now, "thank you" would have to suffice.

The tears in his eyes told me he understood. "I know you wanted to get married. I know this isn't exactly what you had imagined, but I was hoping this could be enough for now. I thought we could be handfasted, as a promise, you know? One day we will have the real thing, you and I." His voice was soft with sincerity. I could tell by the earnest look in his eyes he was genuinely emotionally invested in this idea.

I was bawling. Unbidden, the memory of the difficult, tearful confession which had led him to this conclusion came to mind. The recollection of it washed over me with no care for the present, dragging me under the surface of my mind and transporting me back in time.

❖ ❖ ❖

"Are you going to tell me what you're upset about?" Raven asked with an exasperated sigh.

"Who said I was upset?" I asked, a little too much emphasis on the last word to have fooled anyone, let alone him.

"Your behaviour and body language," he commented dryly, raising a thick ebony eyebrow.

I grumbled under my breath, trying not to be petulant and resentful. Apparently my striving was unsuccessful. I kicked the bottom edge of a piece of furniture in frustration, succeeding only in stubbing my toe. "Ow. Fuck."

"You're right; you're perfectly calm. Zen-like even." He chuckled at his own sarcasm.

I growled a little under my breath, wanting to hit something. He had a way of asking me to look at things I would rather have ignored. Sometimes, he infuriated me. I wished he would let it be, but he would stand there staring at me with an inscrutable knowing gaze until I confessed. I didn't particularly care how much better I always felt afterward. In the moment, being mad felt too good. I was so accustomed to being the rebellious renegade engaged in a battle against cruel authority that I didn't know how to define myself around him. He wasn't a force to be resisted. He was water; his gentle persistence always found an opening. Much like water, the peace and calm he brought was needed. Unfortunately, I didn't know how to appreciate his methods.

"You know, I know what anger looks like from the inside. Believe it or not, I had a real knack for raising hell. I've gotten in fights and torn things up, flipped my finger at authority because I could. I felt small and powerless, you know. I needed to prove myself to the world. I didn't know what to do with all the anger I kept bottled up inside. Whatever it is, I want you to know I understand."

I sighed, my defiant stance defeated, shoulders slumped inward upon themselves. Without the bulwark of my anger, I was vulnerable and scared — a place I didn't like to be. "It's nothing."

He took a step forward, capturing me with his gaze.

*"Clearly, it is **something** if you're so upset about it. Have you ever considered the radical possibility your feelings could be valid?"* He became pointedly direct when frustrated with me. Damn Aquarians.

"No," I protested, my lower lip trembling with the effort of holding the floodwaters at bay. Nothing in my experience had ever led me to believe anything like **that**. I stared at the floor, rubbing a stray red thread into the floorboards with the toe of my beige Birkenstock sandals.

He stepped forward, opening his arms to me wordlessly. I crumpled into them, defeated. Traitorous tears seeped forth in hot abundance despite my best attempts to hold them at bay. He simply held me, letting me cry. When I recovered enough to breathe normally, he pulled back and looked at me. *"Ready to talk yet?"*

I sighed in resignation. How could he possibly be more stubborn than I? His persistence was maddening and endearing at the same time. I wasn't sure if I wanted to kick him or kiss him. *"Ok, fine."* I groaned, sounding more like a petulant teenager than I had intended.

"Ok...?" He waited for me to continue, with his patient smile.

"It's stupid." I said, trying to tear away from his gaze. He held me there. *"I want a future I can never have. I see all these stupid commercials with happy families, and I want what they have. I want kids and a messy house. I want happily ever after. But happily ever after is not for me; it's for other people. I don't deserve such an ending."*

He pulled me into a sudden hug, burying his face into my hair and sighing deeply. The sigh was not a sign of exasperation as much as a sound which spoke of sympathetic pain. The fierce-

ness of his embrace told me he was endeavouring not to cry. "You deserve all the happiness in the world; I only wish I could give it to you. Maybe..." he trailed off.

"No," I said vehemently, looking up into his face. I pulled his head toward mine so he was looking in my eyes. I shook my head for added emphasis. "No maybes; I don't want anyone else. I want you. I would sooner live a life of blessed singleness without you than ever try to live a lie. Ok?"

"Ok." He looked as though he were about to cry.

"Kiss me, please?"

❖ ❖ ❖

My spontaneous reverie faded, returning me to Raven and the clearing. Remembering, I smiled as the sound of footsteps brought me out of my trance state. I looked up at Raven questioningly.

"We need a Priestess to perform the ceremony, don't we?"

I turned to see my sister dressed in her ritual robes, the rich sapphire tones striking against her rose-peach skin and rich auburn hair. She wore all the formal regalia she owned for the occasion. The gesture brought fresh tears to my eyes. They had planned this together. She smiled and took her place by the altar, beckoning us forward.

She began to speak, her clear voice ringing with command. "Love is a gift given from the Gods so we might know ourselves more fully through another's eyes. The sacraments of love are a blessing, never a burden. Love is a partnership of equals, not two becoming one. You cannot possess each other, for you belong to yourselves. You cannot command each other, for your destinies are your own. You cannot change each other, for your differences are the seed and roots of your love. You cannot take from each other, for you can only give what is yours to give."

"You are two who have chosen to join your paths together, guarding each other in times of trouble, and celebrating each other's success in times of joy. This is a pledge to grow together in laughter and in pain. This is a pledge to be the light in the darkness, the guide when all seems lost. This is a promise to meet your disagreements and your quarrels with love; admitting your own mistakes and forgiving them — both those of your own making and your partner's. This is an admission that there are always two; so, too, does the responsibility belong to both of you."

She handed us small scrolls wrapped in ribbon — our vows. He recited his first. "I, Raven, do swear before the Gods, the Elements, and All That Is, to take you, Kara, to my hand, my heart, and my spirit to be my chosen one. I swear to be your partner in growth of mind and spirit; to be your helper, your companion, your lover, your truest friend. I promise you honesty, integrity, and loyalty; to love you wholly and without restraint, in darkness and light, sorrow and joy, in death and beyond, where we shall meet, remember, and love again."

I struggled to read my vows through tears. "I, Kara, do swear before the Gods, the Elements, and All That Is, to take you, Raven, to my hand, my heart, and my spirit to be my chosen one. I swear to be your partner in growth of mind and spirit; to be your helper, your companion, your lover, your truest friend. I promise you honesty, integrity, and loyalty; to love you wholly and without restraint, in darkness and light, sorrow and joy, in life and beyond, where we shall meet, remember, and love again."

Raven and I clasped hands, stretching them so Rhiannon could easily wrap them with the red cords. We gazed into each other's eyes while she tied our hands in literal and proverbial knots. My mind was strangely silent, tears streaming down my cheeks. He was also crying. The sounds of sniffling beside us meant my sister cried as well.

"Where two paths existed, there now is one. May the winds of change always bring the fruit of wisdom to your door. May the fires which burn in your hearth be kindled from passion and love, never anger. May the waters of your hearts flow freely and clear, so you always find yourself blessed by the other's esteem. May the fruits of your labours be doubled in the sharing, and the sorrows halved. May you bring each other joy, always. So mote it be!"

"So mote it be." We echoed Rhiannon's injunction in perfect unison, smiling.

She gave us each a warm hug and kiss before leaving us under the canopy of the tree. The lights blurred in my vision and became a soft ethereal glow, music floating indistinctly through the air. Time stopped, my focus narrowing to his perfect face, haloed in a nimbus of otherworldly light. My heart flooded with a strange mixture of emotions: love, but also thankfulness and awe. I didn't know what to call this feeling I was immersed in; it was the wordless warmth of relaxation, the release of all tension I normally held. It was the feeling of Dorothy coming home from Oz, of waking up to realize it was all a bad dream. Whatever this feeling was, it filled me with a novel sense of peace. He leaned toward me, and my breath caught in my throat, my heart beating faster than a hummingbird's wings, as though we had never kissed before.

"May I?" The quiet, rich tones of his voice sent a shiver of delight down my spine, making my toes curl.

"Yes." I leaned toward him.

9

A STEADY STREAM of synchronicities continued to
appear. Raven's former life was brought up in casual,
innocent remarks by strangers and friends alike, none
of whom knew his connection to me. I felt myself the
object of a particularly cruel case of dramatic irony,
wherein the audience watched the rest of the cast subtly
mock me. I was certain an entire Shakespearean chorus
stood out of sight behind the curtains, tugging at heart-
strings. A best friend from childhood once told me God
was an author, and we all created because we desired to
be like him. Perhaps I should have felt perverse pleasure in realizing I had transitioned from the role of
tragic heroine to comedy star, my personal deity beginning to look more like Shakespeare than Steven King.
Neither was Mercedes Lackey, however, one of the few
authors I would have trusted to play God with my life. I
would much more eagerly have been Vanyel than
Juliet. At least he got his lover back. No matter how

many memories the messages inspired, I continued to feel conflicted about whether or not my relationship with Raven was a delusion spun from my own attachment disorder.

I travelled to stay a few days with some good friends, helping them prepare for a cross-country move. They spontaneously appeared in my life, much like the other strands of my soul family, through the ever-inscrutable threads of destiny. I loved them; they instinctively reminded me of Raven. They were both martial arts students and geeks. We bonded over our shared Buddhism and love of all things nerdy.

I loved her because she reminded me of myself; a gender-fluid girl who wasn't really a girl, while not being a man either — smarter than anyone else around her. I loved him because he was socially awkward and neurologically atypical like me; we understood each other in an effortless way, which only happened with my neuro-divergent spectrum friends. The ex had seen them with the eyes of social stratification acquired in high school, the flawed Darwinian excuse for glorifying narcissistic sociopathy. In his worldview, he was the prom king and they were the wallflowers. I loved them precisely for their awkward authenticity. They were "wallflowers," wild and wonderful like me. I saw them with the eyes of magic; I loved them for their unflinching self-actualization, their awareness of the complex social issues of the world, their compassion, their generosity, their brilliantly creative minds, and radiant spirits.

I loved their incredibly eccentric and eclectic old

rental house; a rambling maze of rooms stuffed with fascinating things like a medieval meal of nested courses or a matroishka doll. If a dragon or a raven had been born as a human, this would have been their house; a hoard of shiny things as carefully curated as a museum. From the East Asian decor to the bookshelves stacked two and three volumes deep to the action figures and entire collections of childhood toys, their treasure trove would have easily shamed Ariel's hideout and The Cave of Wonders.

I spent the day carefully packing their precious treasures, feeling like a kid in a candy shop. Preparing the hoard for transport meant I was privileged to explore every magical inch of it. I was getting paid to indulge my inner geek and hang out with some of my favourite people at the same time. After a delicious dinner, the three of us sat down to rambling conversations and a movie. Spending the night at their house was the adult version of a sleepover. Eventually, however, our rational, adult minds reminded us of the responsibilities of morning. Reluctantly, we said our goodnights and they retired to bed, leaving me alone to ponder. I had a hoard of my own to process.

I stood in the living room, contemplating their Asian philosophy collection. Martial arts books and classic texts lined the short shelves. Here and there, small figurines adorned the shelves: Confucius, Lao Tzu, a set of stern samurai. The martial arts section showcased a complete collection of Bruce Lee books. To my left, a large movie collection lined the walls. Despite the overabundance of visual stimulation, what most captured my attention was the inescapable gravity. The collection contained every one of Raven's martial arts movies, even the rare ones which had to be ordered from China. I was surrounded by images of his former face; the echoes of his old life reverberated around the entire room.

Kung Fu Panda had been our sleepover film, and I felt overwhelmed by feelings I could barely understand. I was struck by the perverse idea I was Ed Gruberman. I had asked the universe, as my *sifu*, for help. In response, the universe had given me a lovely boot to the head. *Accept your destiny*, the Movie Gods said. *Be yourself and become the hero you were born to be*. I had been running from my *unmei* for so long the mere thought of embracing it left my knees knocking and gave my whole body the shakes. *What if I wanted to be my own person, make my own path? What happened to free will? How could a dead man have been my destiny?*

I felt a desperate need to talk to someone, but whom? At home, I would have sat at the kitchen table with my sister until the witching hours of the morning. Here, I would need to rely upon myself. My mind compiled a list of entities I might approach for guidance. Bodhidharma came to mind, but I quickly laughed off the idea. As much as I loved his Tyler Durden approach to enlightenment, he wasn't one for advice. The boot to the head I had already received was much more his style. *Kali, perhaps*? No, she dealt primarily with demons: manifestations of the ego. Close, but not quite. *Tara, then*.

I retired to bed, preparing to enter the other realms.

As I stood in the entrance of the mountaintop monastery She called home, I remembered the first time I had met Tara. It felt like a lifetime ago.

———

My sister and I travelled to California to visit her boyfriend's family for the holidays. His mother was the powerful, cultured, blonde heiress I had always secretly imagined all white mothers to be: one part Martha Stewart and one part Hillary Clinton. She was kind and gentle, but ruthless too. I was immediately intrigued by her. I had never met a woman so domestic and yet so powerful at the same time. She fascinated me. An excellent hostess, she had taken us to a history museum on one of the boring days after Christmas and before New Year's.

We visited an exhibit titled "Treasures from the Roof of the World." The entrance began with a prayer wheel and another ritual relic, whose emanations of power were so strong they nearly knocked me off my feet. The etheric echoes brushed up against my senses with all the force of the Other World. I couldn't imagine how people walked past them so easily, as though they were mere objects of no import. To my senses, they sung with spiritual power. I felt I was standing next to the speakers at a club: the vibrations shaking my whole body, reaching out with electrical arms to tingle the hairs on my neck and make them stand on end. All the molecules of my body resonated with the frequency of the objects. I was a collection of water drops, bouncing and reshaping in response to each subtle vibrational shift. Even with their intensity, another object deeper in the museum pulled my ferrous soul with the strength of a magnet. I had to find whatever was calling me.

Still tuned to the resonance of the ritual tools, I wandered the exhibit in a state of wonder, drinking each object in an inquisitive daze. I found myself drawn to a small golden statue set at eye level behind glass. The script on the figure felt intimately familiar; I was filled with the conviction this script was the writing of the ever-elusive and ephemeral place in the Other I had always considered home. I also always doubted it existed in the flesh. I stood basking in the uncanny recognition of an unnamed something once lost to me, a sense of completion filling my heart. I knew myself whole in both mind and heart — a potent chain of self-criticism rusted away in a single instant. The powerful energy present in the ornate golden statue pulled me in. I was certain this statue was the source of the magnetic disturbance which had drawn me inexorably, realigning all my molecules as it did so. According to the museum label, the statue was a representation of the Goddess Tara: a gift from one of the great Khans to the third Dalai Lama; the text Tibetan.

I heard Her voice in my head, at once strange and instantly familiar. "My child." I recognized Her tone from being claimed by the Phantom Queen before Her. "Mine," Her tone said.

With the mental equivalent of a deep bow, I tried to tactfully decline. "My lady, I already belong to another." I brought the image of the Great Queen to mind.

*She laughed. It was a rich, deep, throaty noise. "That distinction arises in **your** mind." She spoke with the timeless patience of a Goddess who thought Truth painfully obvious and I a particularly silly pup. I wanted to question Her assertion, but the matter of fact way She had spoken forced my mind to admit Her statement made a certain mythological mathematical sense. From the perspective of the soul, **everything** was temporary differentiation, especially as far as Schrödinger had* been concerned. He seemed to know more about the universe than I did.

My conversation with Tara marked the beginning of the rabbit hole of my two-way communication with the universe. The more I approached my spirituality as science, testing each idea against the reality of my experience, the stranger the dialogue became.

———

THE MEMORY FADED, returning me to the present. I hesitated outside Tara's mountain monastery. *Should I enter? Should I wait for Her out here?* Before I made up my mind, I heard a sound behind me. I spun to find Tara standing there, studying me with Her piercing garnet eyes. Tara was an archetype of many faces and forms, shifting shape to embody the concept She represented most at any particular moment. Sometimes She was black, sometimes She was red, other times green, yellow, blue, or white. Today, Her skin was the warm red of sunset. She glowed faintly.

"Liberator," I began, "Granter of boons, please help me. I wish to understand." She smiled gently, with the patience of a parent, waiting for me to continue.

"Great Star, I feel confused." I sighed, struggling to find words to express myself. "The more guidance I seek, the more I feel my life is not my own. I feel as though I am a pawn in a game I can barely understand."

"You are the mover of the pieces."

I shook my head. "I don't understand."

"When you play your role-playing games, are you

not both character and player? And sometimes, are you not also a god when you are the GM?"

I didn't know whether to laugh or cry. Had She compared life to an RPG? And then told me I was the GM?! "What?"

She smiled patiently. "What are the four laws of existence?"

I took a deep breath, reciting from memory. "One: You exist."

She gestured to me with a wave, indicating the obvious truth of my statement. "Continue."

"Two: The All is One and The One is All." *How is any of this relevant to my question?*

She smiled, raising Her perfectly arched eyebrows and tilting Her narrow head to the side. "Yes."

"The total number of conscious minds in the universe is one."

"Yes." She prompted, again waiting for me to continue.

I paused, considering the implications of Erwin's assertion. "So, you're saying free will is an illusion because I chose this?" I failed to comprehend the level of sick self-loathing it would require to be the god who made my world.

"Let us try again. What are the other two laws?"

I sighed with resignation and continued reciting from memory. "Three: you get what you put out. Four: everything else changes. But..."

"Yes," She interrupted excitedly, nodding Her pointy chin.

"If I chose this path as a god, it was with the mind

and knowledge of a god. Now, I am a mortal, with the mind and knowledge of a mortal. How can I accept the choices made for me? As a mortal, have I no choices of my own?"

"Excellent, now you are thinking. When you play your role-playing games, how does it work? Explain this to Me."

"Well..." *Now She wants a lecture on roleplaying?* "First, I create a character..." *Where is this going, and how can it possibly help?*

"Hon, reh! How do you choose what your character will be? Is this character you?"

Sometimes I want to have fun, sometimes they are an echo of an archetype I wish to explore, sometimes I want a particular set of experiences... Huh. "In some ways, yes. Usually, I choose an idea that interests me, a lesson or theme I wish to learn. I give my character flaws and a backstory designed to help me explore this idea."

"Oh! Yes! And when you play this character, is it you, or is it them? Who is conscious, makes the choices, and lives the life?"

I made faces to myself while trying to figure out the answer. *I am all of them, but none of them are entirely me.* "It is me, but not all of me. I am aware of them and their perspective: of their thoughts and feelings. They, however, are not aware of me. The choices they make are their own as are their lives."

"Hon, reh. As below, so above."

I pondered her metaphor, applying parallel structure to better process her meaning. "In other words... my destiny is..." I paused, considering. "...a quest the

'Eternal Me' chose before this life; a lesson my god-self wanted to learn?" I bit my lip for a moment, looking up in thought. "I, the mortal… will explore the chosen theme regardless?" *If I wasn't in control of the story at the moment, what did I have power over?* My eyes widened in sudden comprehension. "How I choose to experience the journey is my choice?"

"Exactly so." She nodded in approval.

"But why did I choose such a twisted path?"

"Hon, reh… Now you have found the real question."

———

IF LIFE WERE A FANTASY NOVEL, each profound personal realization would be followed by instantaneous change. In reality, however, the mind is a funny creature. The mind's primary function is to protect you. The mind also wants to conserve energy. Thus, once a belief has been established, the mind clings to that belief tenaciously, especially when changing the underlying idea represents a fundamental threat to existing mental processes. Although I was intimately familiar with my own rhythms of change and adjustment, the challenges in my path still frustrated me. I didn't trust myself to be the sort of god I needed in my life. I also knew that I was the only god I was going to get.

To answer my question, I needed to find the origin of my path, the place my quest began. As much as I distrusted myself, I couldn't quite believe the Eternal Me was cruel enough to choose my course without a good reason. I had to trust She knew the outcome and was in accord with said conclusion. If nearly two decades of trying to make peace with the idea of Raven and I never physically being together in this life hadn't already happened, it never would. *If my god-self is content with the ending of my story, then She must know something I don't. And if my happy ending requires me to be physically reunited with Raven in this lifetime, then my god-self's acceptance implies a happy ending is at least possible if not probable.*

10

My client, Joan, was crying.

"I don't usually let people see this. I'm not used to letting others see me cry. But you seem to bring it out in me, like it's safe to be emotional around you." She sniffled, dabbing at her blue eyes. "It's been ten years since Michael died, and it hasn't gotten any easier. He was the love of my life. After he passed, I locked myself up here talking to him with my pendulum." She indicated her garret room with a sweep of her sparkly, dragon-clawed hand, the purple of her nails a striking contrast to the peachy bisque of her skin. "Eventually, he made me stop. He didn't think spending so much time with him was healthy for me. But I can't imagine being happy without him. He's the only one who was ever right for me. You're so young, you probably couldn't understand."

Michael himself sat in the chair next to me; a tall, strong, white mountain man with a thick walnut beard.

He sat, watching her with an expression I could interpret easily. At her last statement, he looked at me, raising a bushy grey-brown eyebrow. I might be able to hide my hole from the living, but the dead could always tell. I was glad he couldn't tell her; I wasn't prepared to discuss Raven with her. Family friend or not, I didn't trust her enough. To be honest, I don't trust *anyone* enough to talk about him. I stared at the water glass in my hand, pretending a calm indifference I didn't feel. *No, I don't know the first thing about unhealthy love affairs with dead men or their well-meaning attempts to protect us from ourselves,* I thought, drifting backwards through time with the magic of memory.

———

I STOOD in the centre of my bedroom, surrounded by candles; the quarters had been called, the circle cast. I was Between the Worlds. An eerie sanguine glow suffused the room beyond the golden ring of light in which I stood. The crimson hue matched my mood. Perhaps a normal person would have paused to reconsider the repercussions of their actions, but I've never been capable of normal; passing for human is the most I can manage. I drew the knife I brought into circle specifically for tonight's ritual. My usual dull-bladed ceremonial instrument would not suit my purposes; I needed something far sharper tonight. I quickly stabbed the blade into the tip of my index finger, watching the blood well up in a beautiful crimson bubble. Picking up more candles, I anointed each one with my blood. The

Wiccan Priestess I studied under would have disapproved; white witches usually did. Most Wiccans don't understand the power of blood magic; they fear it.

There is wisdom in their trepidation; blood magic is potent stuff. Then again, perhaps their superstition is pure racism. Modern magery is divided sharply along colonialist lines. Eurocentric traditions, especially those who draw their essences from Catholic ritual, are the heart of Neo-Paganism. These traditions fancy themselves the descendants of remote country folk who, when confronted with the Holy Roman Empire, chose to preserve their traditional indigenous beliefs in private. In truth, a great many members of family traditions exist, but are not considered part of the generally accepted traditions. Most of the self-proclaimed "reconstructionalist" and Neo-Pagan traditions follow practices more closely related to the secret societies and mystery traditions of Europe — Masonry, The Gnostics, and the Golden Dawn — than traditional indigenous practices. Fam-trads tend to have more in common with other practitioners of witchcraft: a diverse diaspora of indigenous cultural traditions which modernity — and Christianity in particular — had attempted to displace. Our ways are often of root and stem, blood and hair. Their ways are pomp and circumstance. As a rebellious renegade who prefers to snub tradition, I chose to mix the elegant drama of Neo-Pagan theatrics and the blood magic of my ancestors. The paradoxical juxtaposition of old and new suited me.

My final task in preparation was summoning the gods, so I did. I stood in the centre of my circle, arms outstretched. Picking up each candle in turn, I spoke in a clear, commanding tone.

"Anubis, The Jackal Headed, Carrier of Souls to the Underworld, hear me. Guide, Guardian, Judge, hear me now." I lit the first candle, clearly picturing Him in my mind's eye: His deep golden obsidian skin; long canine snout; and tall, mountainous ears.

"Kali, Force of Time, Mother of All, hear me. Creator, Destroyer, Protector, hear me now." I lit the second candle, focusing intently on Her form: Her rich, night-sky skin, so black it was blue; Her thick ebony hair; Her sanguine smile.

I continued, naming the death gods I knew — save one — as well as others I had researched specifically for tonight. After all, just because Raven had placed a geas upon me, preventing me from committing suicide, didn't mean he could stop a god or goddess from taking me to the Afterlife. When I finished, the room felt over-crowded. The heat from the candles began to make me sweat. I should have been awed or intimidated in the presence of so many death deities. Instead, I felt deter-mined — and slightly nauseated.

"Gods and Goddesses of the Underworld, Lords and Ladies of the Dead, I invite Thee here this night to strike a bargain. Whoever among Thee has strength to kill me, may take my soul. I offer Thee my blood as proof and seal. Take me, I will be Thine." I gestured dramatically with a sweep of my velvet clad arm.

The silence was deafening. Their penetrating gazes were even more discomfiting than the stares of a crowd of millions. I noticed one or two deities shake Their heads and immediately leave. I was worried about Their reluctance; my Goddess was not known for Her forgiveness. Only an extremely strong (or mad) deity would be willing to fight Her for my soul, but surely at least one of Them was up to it. Maybe I should have invited Hel. I might have idly fantasized about servitude as a Valkyrie, but I did not desire to spend eternity in service to the pantheon worshipped by the perpetrators of the Porajmos. The Norse gods may not have been directly responsible for the Great Devouring, but there were still those hidden among the Asatru who maintained Nazi ideas of purity. Suicidal I may be, but I still possessed some modicum of self-preservation, even if the only shred remaining was the survival instinct of my ancestors. Between the Viking raids on the Isles of my father's people and the all-too-recent genocide of my mother's familia, the Asatru were best avoided. *No, thank you.* I did not trust any of the Norse pantheon, except Loki. I knew He, at least, did not share their ethnocentric tendencies.

I knew the gods were deliberating and would not be hurried, no matter how desperately I might wish otherwise. I sat in the centre of the circle and waited. Hours passed. As immortal beings, the Gods have Their own sense of time. An eternity to us may be mere moments to Them. Demoralized and disappointed, I went to bed. The Gods alone would decide whether I waited all night. My bargain had been struck; nothing I did now would change anything.

Morning came with no obvious reply. I rose from my bed, despondence deepening into despair, stubbornly prepared to wait. My first step made it painfully clear I was unwell: my body was sluggish, my head throbbed, my skin felt too tight.

The next thing I remember is standing at the discharge window of the Emergency Clinic, talking to the nurse. Uninsured and only temporarily employed, being there didn't make any financial sense to me

"We've called someone to pick you up. You shouldn't be driving with a temperature of 106. In fact, we're not sure how you managed to drive yourself here. Here are your prescriptions. Get these filled, go home, get some rest. Talk to your loved ones. If you wake up tomorrow, you'll live. Good luck." I was stunned. I'd never heard a medical professional admit life was out of their hands before. Nor had I ever been told I was going to die. Things were looking up.

Fever induced delirium does funny things. In my case, funny things mean permanent realm bleedover. Without my brain's ability to separate the aggregate sensory streams from all the realms, I was caught Between the Worlds in a semi-permanent state of flux.

I woke to find the chair from my bedroom table beside my bed. The Phantom Queen sat there, tapping Her foot. My feverish brain struggled to make sense of the strange scene. I had never seen Her during daylight before. I was accustomed to meeting Her in the realm of Eternal Night, surrounded by the trappings of Death. The Phantom Queen's somber appearance was incongruous against the backdrop of my sunny, buttercup-clad walls; She was Lily Munster appearing suddenly on Fraggle Rock. I had never seen a Goddess tap Their feet, or wear shoes. *Shit*, I thought.

The Phantom Queen was an ancient pan-Celtic Goddess of changing forms. Sometimes She wore the dark skin and bright eyes of the early Bretons; sometimes the small, dark features of the Welsh; sometimes She was a ruddy Scottish lass; sometimes She wore the pale skin and red hair of the Irish. Sometimes there was one of Her, and sometimes there were three. Unlike other triple goddesses, whose faces were formed by patriarchy and were thus tied to reproductive roles, The Great Queen or Phantom Queen (depending upon your translation or Her mood) was a force of sovereignty — all Her aspects were the fierce warrior women once common amongst the peoples of the world. Usually, Her clothing matched the people of the historical period She was representing.

Today, She was the picture of Scottish fury; Her thick amber curls corralled in a fiercely braided fauxhawk that continued down her spine. Her eyes were bottomless pools of inky blackness; She was the cold void of deep space. She sported a classically British suit: a close-cropped blazer whose low scoop-neck revealed a scalloped, collared blouse, paired with narrow, pinstripe pants. A pair of sturdy yet stylish buckled boots completed the all-black ensemble. I had never seen Her wear modern clothes before. This did **not** bode well.

"You ungrateful little *ɹoith*." Her face was a mask of fury. *Yep. Not going to end well.* She was breaking out the Gaelic curse words. "You have no idea the trouble I've been through to clean up the mess you made here. Do you not realize how hard I have worked to keep you alive? Who do you think has been protecting you your whole life? Now you want to throw all MY efforts away in some misguided temper tantrum? You think this is about some geas placed on you by your beloved? This is bigger than the two of you. Get over yourself, little girl. You have a lot left to do before it's your time." She leaned closer, fixing me with Her timelessly inscrutable gaze. Her eyes were lasers, boring into my soul and branding me as Hers. "You live at my mercy. Remember that." Then She was gone.

If I thought Raven would be indulgent or tolerant of my suicide attempt, I was mistaken. Apparently, the dead don't approve of mélange. His face was a mixture of pain and anger: eyes wide, brows pinched, generous mouth compressed in a tight line. I was looking at a stranger. Accustomed to his gregarious playful nature, I was shocked to see him so subdued. He looked ready to cry.

"Kara..." Raven trailed off, running his fingers through his sable hair from forehead to crown. He stared at the ceiling in exasperation, shaking his head. When he finally looked back at me, his face was filled with bitter disappointment. "What were you thinking?" he asked, his broken voice barely above a whisper.

The lead weight of guilt filled my stomach, pulling me under the surface of my own emotions and drowning me. "I wanted to be with you. I thought..." I trailed off, uncertain of my conviction, which felt so strong in the solitude of sorrow but was now significantly shrunken.

He paced back and forth, looking as though he wanted to pull his hair out or rip off his own head, but wasn't sure which one to do first. Finally, he took a deep, shuddering breath and turned face at me again. "You thought, after I had bargained with the Queen of Phantoms for your life, you would throw everything away? What, did you think I would be *happy* if you were dead?" His thick brows were drawn down; heavy, dark thunderclouds creased together in the middle. A deluge of tears threatened to flood forth from his eyes.

"Trading your soul to the highest bidder was the answer? What did you hope to accomplish with your bargain? Did you imagine we could be dead happily ever after? This isn't Shakespeare. That's not how it works!" The torrential downpour streamed down his cheeks now. Every inch of his gaze was accusatory. I felt it spear through my chest, locking my heart and lungs in an iron grip. I could barely breathe.

"You, of all people, should know better. How many restless dead have you helped cross over? How many hungry ghosts have you saved? Did you not, for one moment, think leaving your life in such a way would doom you to suffering?" He sighed, frowning and shaking his head for emphasis.

"Imagining souls were sellable things to be bought and traded — which is another fallacy — did you even consider what such a bargain meant? Suppose some god of the Underworld accepted your offer and seized you as Their own. How would I ever see you again? I'm an actor and a martial artist, not a necromancer priest! Did you stop to think what eternity might have been like for me without you? Did you not realize I would have been unable to move on into a new life, never knowing where you were?" He sobbed angrily.

I wanted only to make his tears stop. Knowing I was the cause of his suffering twisted the spear further into my chest impaling me to drown with my sorrow.

"Did you consider *anything* outside of yourself? You think you're the only one suffering here, but you're not. Do you think I enjoy being dead? Every time you cry because I'm not there to hold you, it kills me a little more. Do you know how devastating it is to be unable to comfort you? How many nights I've watched you sleep, keeping you safe, because I couldn't lie there with you? This isn't fun for me either, love."

He resumed pacing and running his hand through his hair. I waited and watched, sick with worry. Finally he stopped, turning to face me again. "I love you. I love you too much to be the reason for your pain. You have a full life ahead of you, and I intend for you to live it."

I was crying. "What are you saying?" I was afraid I would puke at any second. There were spots at the corners of my eyes, and I fought to breathe through the pain. *How can he be doing this to me?*

"I'm saying, this relationship is over. I love you. I will always love you. But I cannot and will not watch you destroy your life for me. It's wrong. I never should have kissed you. This is wrong. I'm sorry." His voice was sharp with anguish, but anger lurked in the corners of his storm-darkened eyes.

My sadness smouldered into a fiery inferno of rage. I needed to wound him as deeply as he wounded me.

Doesn't he understand he is the centre of my universe? I ripped off my handfasting ring and threw it at him. I'll always remember the hollow ringing sound the metal band made as it clinked and rolled on the floor, and the look of pain in his eyes. "Fine. Fuck you, then." I wanted a clever retort, some Gemini-inspired witticism which would emotionally destroy him, but I didn't have anything left. My heart collapsed into a black hole whose event horizon was slowly spreading outward and spaghettifying me.

I turned and ran.

11

AFTER NOT EATING for three days, you acquire a feeling of powerful immortality. On the first day, you're hungry, but the urge is ignorable. On the second day, your stomach is a separate entity, a gnawing monster threatening to rip out your spine for nourishment. By the third day, you have started to come through the need to eat. You have begun to realize how much time is wasted in our societal indulgence of consumption as a community experience. You start to consider others weak for the need to consume. You have begun to believe you are better than they are.

I taught myself the secret art of starvation, eating enough to fool onlookers when pressed. My growing distance from food became a blanket of detachment which separated me from my emotions with blessed relief. Disassociation had always been one of my super-powers. Apathy was merely the next level. I might be trapped in my life, but I sure as hell didn't have to live it. I hid behind my mask of perfection, sinking deeper and deeper into my personal abyss. I distanced myself from others with practical excuses, letting the other girls — Emma and Gwen — go off to group dates and parties without me. I was alone, as I preferred.

I was always aware of the ever-present darkness inside me: my laughter was forced and stilted, my smiles faked. The inner fire I possessed since childhood had been smothered. I was a poor approximation of a young adult, an awkward jilted mummery. For most of my life I felt painfully aware of how different I was — my humanity nothing more than a performance necessary for my continued survival. This distance, however, was different than my previous experiences. Others my age were full of life, hope, and promise. I, however, was only alive because it was required. I drew my darkness around me like armour, trying to push the world away. I dressed in black and went to Goth night at the club, comforted by the culture of others who romanticized death. They understood having a black hole for a heart.

I was far enough into my eating disorder to feel superior to humanity, but not far enough to have grown a layer of peach fuzz when Raven intervened. I returned home late one night to find him waiting for me in the driveway. From a living ex, this behaviour bordered uncomfortably on stalking. From a dead one it was positively possessive. I stepped sideways into the Other, prepared for a confrontation.

"What are you doing here?" I placed my hands on my hips, staring him down. The forgotten fire in my core re-ignited, sleeping coals stoked to fury. I was not amused.

"You haven't revoked my permission to enter." His voice was dry and humourless.

"I can fix that." I growled, glowering. The coals grew brighter.

"As you wish." I couldn't place his tone, but I didn't exactly try to. I was too incensed at his gall.

The smouldering embers caught fire. *How dare he use movie quotes against me. Especially **that** quote.* "You don't get to say shit like that anymore, asshole. Why. Are. You. Here." My every breath fuelled the fiery inferno, the flames leaping higher and higher. I advanced toward him with angry steps timed to each word, poking my index finger at him. He was only a spirit and I was a medium. I was the boss here.

"I know you're not eating."

"So?" I didn't need to eat. Eating was for mere mortals.

"Eat or Die." Once, I would have found his ironic smile charming. Now I simply found his expression infuriating.

"As if you care." I wished my words were nails I might use to impale him to a tree. The blazing maelstrom spiralled out of control, spreading out of my core and into my limbs. My palms began to burn.

"I do care." Sorrow and regret choked his voice.

"You've got a fucked up way of showing it, buddy. What, you go around breaking up with girls for their own good? Because you care so much?"

I stood at a distance that would have once felt intimate. Now the proximity felt painful. I wanted to punch him as hard as I could, but also wanted him to hug me. I hated feeling so conflicted. I wanted to hate him for having this power over me. Our breakup would be so much easier to handle if I could only hate him. I tried to blink away the tears threatening me with their traitorous presence. *Not now, Riordan. Stay cool,* I told myself, digging my fingernails into my palms and biting the inside of my cheek, using the pain as a focus. I would not cry; he didn't deserve to see me cry. I could tell I had wounded him with my angry words. *Good.*

"Kara, please don't do this." His calmness infuriated me even more.

"No, don't **you** do this, Raven! Don't come here and act like you care about me. You left me when I was at rock bottom and now you want come back like some guardian angel? And you call me selfish? How dare you!" I would have emphasized my point by pounding on his chest with my fists if he hadn't caught my wrists. His touch only enraged me further, feeding the conflagration. I screamed incoherently at him — a wordless howl of pain and rage as the pyre consumed me. He stood there silently, holding my hands to prevent me from hitting him. My fury spent, I stood sobbing. The flames receded to dim embers in my chest. Defeated, I hung my head and refused to look at him.

After a tearful eternity, he finally spoke. "Kara." He wanted me to meet his eyes; I continued to stare at our feet. A stray red string lay tangled between our matching Birkenstock sandals. I wanted to destroy the thread and our footwear. I wanted to destroy every-thing. "Kara, please look at me."

"No." I wanted to punish him. I wanted him to prove he cared for me. I wanted to make him mad, to hurt him. I wanted to cry in his arms and discover the events of the past few months were nothing but a stupid nightmare. I wanted him to know how badly he had hurt me, and I wanted him to pay for it.

"Please."

Sullenly, I met his eyes to find he was crying too.

"Please, Kara. I need you to eat."

"Why?" I wasn't ready to relinquish my defiance. He might see how vulnerable I was without it.

"Because I love you. Because I want you to live."

"Prove it," I demanded, icily. Words were nice and all, but as my birth parents had been so fond of saying, actions speak louder. I needed action, not words.

Raven reached into his shirt and pulled out my ring, strung on a cord. "There's more." He took the band off the necklace and offered it to me. I took the ring from him wordlessly, sliding it back on my finger. I gestured toward the house.

Raven followed me inside, up the narrow winding staircase to my crowded garret bedroom. Having not invested the time or energy to create an astral temple attached to my abode, the Otherworld version was simply a paler reflection of my actual room. Other than my bed, the only available seating in my messy space was a small chair. Unwilling to have him sit on my bed or do so myself because of the intimacy such a seating arrangement implied, I indicated the floor. He sat across from me in an effortless echo of our first meeting, still as serpentine as always. Though my posture still hadn't improved, this time I was also wearing all black.

"I'm sorry I hurt you. You're right; I left you in a terrible place. We each said and did shitty things to each other. We need to have an honest conversation, or this relationship will never work. We've become toxic; it's not healthy for either one of us. That's not what I wanted. That's not what this relationship is supposed to be." He paused, waiting for me to respond.

"You were right. I'm sorry. I was being selfish, and I did think I was the only one in pain. I didn't realize you were suffering, too. I wasn't trying to hurt you. I'm just so tired of being heartbroken. I thought our incongruent timelines were a mistake; it was wrong for you to be dead and me still alive. I thought I could fix our lifelines; reset our reincarnation timelines to match. It was a stupid, juvenile blunder. But I had to try. Because I refuse to accept that this," I paused, gesturing to indicate our ephemeral interaction, "is all we get. I want more." I twisted the hem of my skirt in my hand, trying to maintain eye contact. Raw honesty is terrifying.

"I understand. I want more too. Which is why I've been working so hard to find a solution. I didn't want to tell you in case I didn't find anything, but I did."

His words took a minute to sink in. "Wait; back up. What?" I dropped the fabric, leaning toward him.

"I found a solution."

A normal human being would have leaned over and

kissed him or squealed excitedly. I was too emotionally stunned to do anything. My heart couldn't process what my brain was hearing. His slow, measured tone didn't exactly bespeak excitement, either, but caution.

"Explique s'il vous plaît?" I reverted to my childhood French. *At least I didn't use sign language.*

"I found a way to come back. From what I understand, it's sort of an exchange process."

"So, there's… what, a used body dealership, and you're going to go get the best possible model?" Surely, as a medium I would have heard about this "other method" before.

"Not exactly, no. I don't comprehend it completely. From what I understand, the process is more like an organ donor list." He laughed weakly.

"Oh." I said blankly, as if his statement explained anything at all. "Ok…" *How does one become matched with another body? Do they do blood typing or genetic analysis? Is there a waiting list?* I made a mental note to do some research later.

"Sometimes people don't want to live anymore, you know? They might go into a coma, or be otherwise dead, although their body remains alive. Sometimes, under the right circumstances, someone else can step in." His vague, uncertain smile was far from convincing.

"Ok…" *How have I never heard of this?! I need to do more research.* "So… what does this mean for us, exactly?" I tried to wrap my heart and head around the idea of him in a new body. *What will he look like? Will he even be a he again?*

"It means we'd have to find each other all over again, but that's the easy part. We've already succeeded once. Besides, we are bound together by strange forces, you and I. Death cannot stop true love..." he quoted with a small wink and a playful smile, daring me to finish the line.

"All it can do is delay it for a while." Feeling was softening the edges of the ice covering my heart. It would be the movie quote that got me. *Of course.* "If love proves real, and two people are meant to be together..."

"Nothing can keep them apart. Jyun Fan. The red string of fate." He was grinning from ear to ear.

"I love you." *Am I laughing or crying? Laugh-crying?* The system lag between my ears and heart had finally caught up. We might yet have a future together. The dark abyss in my heart held the tiniest glimmer of hope. I prayed the black hole had collapsed under its own weight and would be unable to snuff out the small spark.

"I love you." We leaned toward each other, drawn by a mutual gravitational pull. "May I?" he asked.

"Please."

This kiss was not gentle. Too much had passed between us. This kiss was fierce with sorrow, longing, and relief. On some level, we knew this kiss meant farewell, at least for a time. He carried me to the bed, and we spent the night saying goodbye.

In the morning when I awoke, he was gone. The sun streamed brightly through my bedroom windows, illuminating a sheet of paper on the table next to my bed. I couldn't imagine what it had cost him energetically to leave a physical message in the mortal realm. The ability to directly manipulate the physical realm was typically limited to extremely strong hauntings, usually those traumatized and violent souls who were tied to a specific location. Incredibly intense emotions and a powerful psychic field were required to even touch physical objects; creating a separate item out of one's own spiritual essence was an act of legend. He would have had to literally pull out a piece of his immortal soul to create such a manifestation. Tears streaming down my face, I read the note.

"Just so you never forget. No matter how many times you try to hurt me, no matter what you do. Even if you push me away, or tell me to fuck off, I'll still be over here, loving you. Nothing will change that, ever. See you soon, my love." The note was signed with a raven sketch.

I keep the piece of paper on my altar in a box with other talismans.

———

I FORGOT DESPITE HIS NOTE, I thought with a flash of anger at myself as I returned to the present. The corners of my eyes began to burn, unshed tears struggling to be free. I blinked furiously and drank some more water from the glass in my hand, trying to wash the tears away. Michael was still watching me with a knowing expression. Damn insightful ghosts. Joan got up to use the bathroom, needing to retreat for a moment. She had confessed her deepest wound, after all. I felt a little duplicitous sitting here avoiding mine.

"It ain't gonna go away by ignorin' it, girl. You got a powerful loveache there. What scares you 'bout it?"

I averted my gaze, pretending not to hear him. This rarely worked, but I didn't want to have this conversation.

"I know you kin hear me," he continued, his stare unrelenting. "You don't owe me any answers; I don't know you from Adam. But seeing you sit here, with a hurt as powerful as my Joan's, makes a man need to ask. If your'n is alive, why ain't you with 'im?"

I shrugged in response, refusing to look at him. Traitorous tears trickled down my cheeks, hot and salty. *Why had I given up on my love for Raven? How had I allowed my inner critic to silence and suppress my certainty? What happened to my hope; the future of a promise together with Raven? When did I abandon my quest?* In the perfect wisdom of hindsight, my denial was obvious — a pot of boiling water atop a stove.

I had been an oblivious frog, merely enjoying a nice warm bath. My mind had completely cooked me before I became aware of what was happening. Now I realized what my reality reflected as Michael's simple statement of fact wounded me.

I had been living as though my entire experience was a lie; as though Raven and his reincarnation were mere figments of my imagination. If this premise was a product of reality, rather than a product of my own internal gaslighting, Michael would have said as much. I knew his integrity from Joan's stories — Michael was not a man who lied. Even if he had been, my own internal truth sensors were telling me otherwise; his words were a punch to my solar plexus. Goosebumps blossomed on my skin, waves of energy washing out from my heart chakra and over my skin in cascades, hair standing on end. I shivered.

12

MICHAEL'S WORDS HAUNTED ME. Why had I given up? Possessed by a powerful need for answers, I sought the only person who would have them: myself. In the bottom of a large, clear storage container, underneath my high school graduation gown and senior girls t-shirt, next to the hairbrush and stuffed E.T., I found my journals. The melancholy malaise they contained brushed at my senses. I knew why I had avoided reading the volumes for so long. You didn't even need psychometry to feel the waves of angst pouring off them. The words within were written in anguish.

Page after page was filled with the unbearable ache for Raven, interspersed with hopeful passages of excitement and expectation over seeing him soon. The former were painful to witness; the latter broke my heart. Every time teenage me had written of seeing him on a certain date, her excitement was so profoundly palpable that all she had been able to write was a simplistic "Yay

yay yay!!" Watching dates pass by without any comment reminded me of the stoicism I once possessed. Nowhere had she written of the bitter pangs of disappointment. I didn't need her words to remind me, however; I was all too familiar with the feeling. With the perspective of time, I knew she would gradually stop looking for him. She would create a rule: "You are allowed to hope, but never to expect." Hope may have been the force which gave me wings to fly, but expectation was surely the planet whose persistent pull grounded me.

I remembered the awful pendulum swing between hope and despair. Her poetry spoke of the pain of temptation, knowing the bliss of time spent in his embrace would be followed by the ache of separation. She spoke of her love for him with a tone I recognized as addiction. With the insight of recovery, she knew each moment of peace was costing her. *"Reluctantly I awaken from the euphoria of your presence and remind myself of the price to fall into those eyes. It is all too easy."*

Her journal entries were unfailingly full of pain, including the music lyrics.

"Pride can stand a thousand trials...the strong will never fall, but watching stars without you my soul cried... heaving heart is full of pain... oh, oh, the aching." A decade had passed since I had heard this song. Despite the distance of years, I could hear Des'ree's voice as clearly as if the song were currently playing. I remembered how the song felt written for me, as though Des'ree saw straight into my heart and put my pain into words. I was comforted knowing someone else could under-

stand. This song perfectly described the hole in my heart.

Drawn by sorrow, I read with heavy heart, remembering each moment.

"I turn upon fate and laugh, for though I am a mere mortal, Love is my shield; belief my sword. There is no battle I will not win. There are no trials I will not stand; the strength in me will never fail. Push me to death, I laugh at you. Shove me to Hades and I shall smile. Nothing can stop me; neither foe nor friend.

"No water will drown our love, not fire burn it. No air can snuff it out, nor earthquakes sunder it. If I have to dig a hole to the other side of the universe, walk to the moon, and paint the stars with my blood, I will. So laugh if you will — I shall laugh last."

Despite her sorrow, she was singularly possessed of a powerful conviction to find him. Her audaciously wilful spirit leapt off the page, reminding me I had once felt fearless. Her plea to me finally tore my heart open.

"No-one knows what our future holds. Except for you. I wish I could ask you. Is my love strong enough to create a miracle?" Her earnest certainty in me felt profoundly misplaced. She had entrusted me with her most precious dream and sacred mission. I failed her; I abandoned her quest. *How could I? What had I been thinking?!* A tidal wave of guilt washed over me, pulling me under the surface of self-loathing and smashing me against the rough rocks of criticism and despair. *How had I changed from a girl so defiantly devoted to a girl who settled for a second-rate cosplay of love? Somewhere along the way, I betrayed myself, but where? And why?*

I dove into my mind palace, heading directly for help. Eager for answers, I sped through the entry sequence, completing the elevator ride in record time. As soon as the doors opened, I raced across the canyon, pausing only to unlock the chain-link fence and verify my identity so that the giant gear-shaped door could slowly open. The damn thing took forever.

"Hello, Madame." I dashed past my first guide, acknowledging its presence with a quick wave. As turbulent as I felt, I trusted one spirit guide implicitly: Dr. Truth. I stood before the door to her office, knocking on the bubbles of the mechanical glass which provided privacy while also allowing light to enter. I waited patiently for her to open the old metal door.

No one interrupted Dr. Truth. She was a multidimensional being from elsewhere in the universe: enigmatic, powerful, and incredibly old. She reminded me of the Mrs. Ws. in Madeline L'Engle's works, specifically a mixture of Mrs. Which and Mrs. Who. She didn't often speak unless asked direct questions, usually preferring to communicate through body language. When she did speak, her words were always wise. I suspected she had once been a star. Like all spirit guides, Dr. Truth chose the form she wore for me from my memory, selecting a body both symbolically appropriate and suited to her personality. She had chosen the form of my favourite abolitionist and donned a white lab coat.

After some time, the door opened. Dr. Truth regarded me shrewdly, narrowing her expressive amber eyes and pursing her lips into a tight, narrow line. She shook her head and opened the door wider, gesturing for me to enter. I headed for the comfortably over-stuffed green couch. Dr. Truth closed the door, the small bell on it singing quietly. She sat in an office chair, rolling it closer to the couch. Normally, Dr. Truth smiled when she rolled around in her office chair, a rich bronze copper flushing her broad brown cheeks with the timeless enjoyment of youth. Today, she frowned, her face a thundercloud. *Oh, boy. No pressure.*

"You in the valley," she said, dismissing my unasked question with a wave of her dexterous hand. "Chile, you got doubt and self-hatred written all over your face. Out with it." I suspected Dr. Truth had borrowed some of her mannerisms from memories of my Aunt Gladys, one of the few trustworthy adults in my turbulent and traumatic childhood. The no-nonsense way she spoke was straight out of my Aunt's book. Neither woman tolerated any bullshit. This attitude put my fears at ease. Charlatans and abusers hid behind prevarication and pomp, polishing your ego like pick-up artists after a mark. The more direct someone was, the more I trusted them. Dr. Truth, much like Aunt Gladys, never sweet-ened the truth — she believed in serving up every bitter, heaping spoonful you deserved. As painful as her insights were, they were equally necessary. She wielded words with a surgeon's skill — cutting to the core of an issue to facilitate future healing. The truth may hurt now, but it was always wise medicine.

"I feel as if I have betrayed myself, Dr. Truth. I abandoned the single most important quest in my life." My voice was heavy with self-recrimination.

She pursed her lips and gave me "the look." It was the same look Aunt Gladys wore when she saw right through your shit and you had better 'fess up 'fore she called you out on it.

"It feels like I did," I mumbled dejectedly, feeling petulant and childish.

"Hmmph," she vocalized in a perfect imitation of my Aunt, her shoulders rising and falling with the sound. "Alright then." She shrugged and turned, as if to dismiss me and go back to work. It was, of course, a ploy. Her imaginary indifference was merely a tactic designed to draw the confession out of me. She knew I needed to talk, but she also knew I was recalcitrant when it came to talking about my feelings. By pretending she had more important things to do, she could provoke me to communicate. This method worked so well it had become a routine for us. I would enter her office reluctant, she would feign apathy; I would confess.

"But..." I interrupted her.

She paused, regarding me out of the corner of her eye. She tilted her head in question, waiting for me to continue.

I sighed and shook my head. "You're saying I didn't?"

She laughed, one slender, sepia hand slapping her knee for good effect. "Oh, chile. I never say. You do the sayin'. I ask." *She has a point.*

I covered my face with my palm, taking a ragged breath. "Ok. So... I didn't give up?"

She nodded, gesturing with her graceful hand for me to continue.

"Then why does it feel as if I did?"

She raised her eyebrows in silent response to my question and gestured to the couch in a nonverbal invitation for me to lie down. I would find the answers I sought only within myself. I closed my eyes. Down the rabbit hole I went.

A series of scenes flashed through my mind; paradoxically instantaneous and infinitely long. Time has no meaning in the other realms.

I found a forgotten dream first. I stood on the second-story balcony of an apartment, facing a tree. The bare winter branches were decked with an inky blackness, which resolved into the largest parliament I had ever seen. There were hundreds of birds; enough to replace each fallen leaf. I longed to touch them. Naturally, they were out of reach. Any movement I made toward them would only startle the gathering, eliciting squawks and wing flaps, flight if I persisted.

Strange, small flowers lay at my feet. Curious, I bent to pick one up, but the minuscule buds slipped through my fingers. I persisted. My focus narrowed as I took slow, deliberate breaths until nothing but the bloom existed. Gently, I lifted the blossom's fragile form into my hand. The flower's fragrance was sweet and spicy, elusive rather than cloying. The parliament sounded excited by my actions, their timid calls growing into the raucous exultation of found treasure. One of their number flew to the railing, regarding me with knowing eyes. I sensed a familiarity in its gaze and found myself lost.

As surely as if I had summoned him, the large black bird leapt into my hand, landing deftly. He began to peck at the flower, and I was surprised by his gentleness. His beak was meant to rip through flesh. Ravens were omnivores, after all. Despite this, his touch was as gentle and deft as a butterfly's. I marvelled at his dexterity, noticing he was careful not to bite. As though he could hear my thoughts, the bird laughed, throwing his head back in a throaty gurgle. He became a man. I **had** known those eyes. As we embraced, I heard the disembodied echo of my own voice narrating.

"Do not hunt the Raven - invite him in with a meal prepared. So I begin the hunt for myself, my god within, and the girl I once buried."

Before I had time to fully reflect on the meaning of those words, the scene changed.

Kwan Yin sat serenely on her lotus, pouring forth liquid from the vase in her hand. A jewel-toned dragon slept, coiled peacefully under her. Ethereal zither music filled the air, and butterflies danced among currents of incense. Her realm was a radiant mix of colours, pastels and richer tones softly combined. The artist in me longed to take a photo of Her realm and recreate it in the physical. I wanted to spend eternity here.

The goddess looked up from Her reverie, smiling. She extended one slender, seashell-hued hand toward me in a gesture of welcome, inviting me to sit. The other thousand arms maintained their respective poses. I was fascinated by the effortless way She moved. I was clumsy enough with two arms; moving a thousand with a dancer's easy grace seemed impossible. I suppose I should have knelt before Her, but witches don't kneel to our gods. Instead, I bowed. Bowing felt more culturally appropriate.

"Mother of Mercy, thank you for hearing my cries." I saw the sympathy in Her dark amber eyes, one silvery tear slipping down Her rosy cheek. I found Her gesture reassuring, as though my pain did indeed echo through Her. "I have come to ask for your aid."

She smiled serenely, waiting for me to continue. "Mother of Mercy, I feel so confused." I collapsed into a heap at Her feet. Uncertain, I wrestled with my emotions for some time. My stomach was certain I had eaten my 8lb dumbbells for breakfast and swallowed the skillet along with the eggs for good measure. My heart was a Roman gladiator, shackled in an iron cage and fighting unto death. I wanted to be comforted, but I was convinced I would not ever find any comfort. I didn't deserve comfort. I deserved gods who tested and punished with impunity, not gentle guides to enlightenment. If not to appease the cosmic scales, why else had my life been a trial of torment?

I wanted to ask Her everything: why I deserved such cruelty, what I could possibly do to atone for my unknown sins, and whether I would ever truly be able to be with Raven. I was cowed by the fear of what She might say, however. I wanted Her wisdom, but only if it brought me peace, not the sorrow I was convinced was my fate. I was terrified to discover that such suffering was simply my destiny. I wanted Her to tell me everything would be alright, even though I was certain nothing would ever be.

She watched me for some time, crying quietly. My internal struggle remained subdued. Fists clenched tight and jaw set in a grim line, I tried to be stoic as a Jedi. Kwan Yin simply cried. She tilted Her head to the side while watching me, Her wide brow wrinkling down into a sad frown. When She finally spoke, Her voice was soft and peaceful, the gentle gurgle of a mountain stream. "You are allowed to cry."

I shrugged, chin trembling as the first fat drops fell. She unfolded Her thousand arms in invitation and I let Her hold me, crying as I never had before. I wept thunderstorms in Her lap, curled up upon myself like an infant. She simply held me, rocking me back and forth and singing a sutra in a tongue I didn't know. For the first time in my life, I was with all my sorrow. I let it empty out of me as the walls of the dams I had built finally failed.

All the pain of my past poured forth into Her arms; my anger at my birth parents, my agony over losing my brothers, my longing for Raven. Underneath my various and sundry sorrows lurked the idea I was unworthy of love. Through the entirety of my emotional torment, She surrounded me in Her compassionate embrace. Little by little, the gale force of my turbulent pressure changes began to subside. Sobs became tears. Tears became breathing. Eventually I was spent, breathing deeply in her lap.

She placed one velvety soft, slender hand under my chin, tilting my face and cradling my head as a mother might. "If I give you a gift, and you value the gift, you will keep your prize as an object treasured by you. You will look upon the gift with eyes of gratitude and be blessed for receiving. If I give you a gift and you choose not to receive it, if you complain the present is not what you were expecting, your gift will not be a reward to you but a burden carried out of obligation — which brings only pain." She paused for emphasis, looking into my eyes. "You have been given a gift. Is it your treasure or your burden?"

Realization of her koan unfolded in my heart and mind in a blinding moment of beautiful insight. I understood. A montage of scenes flashed before my eyes: crying because I couldn't go to prom with him, crying because I didn't believe I was beautiful, crying because I was jealous of those who had known him in the flesh, crying because I wanted more. Every date turned into a confession, every bouquet an opportunity for self-flagellation; I had fashioned my love for him into a razor blade and slit my own wrists. I could have been making the memories I so desperately craved instead of feeling sorry for myself. Every step of the way, Raven had tried to give me happiness and joy. Only when my self-obsessed cycle spiralled into suicide had he given up and refused to be part of my toxic fantasy.

Hot tears coursed down my cheeks. I never wanted our relationship to be toxic. I wanted our relationship to be a treasure. I wanted happily ever after. When we'd been together, however, I hadn't been able to appreciate our relationship. I didn't know how to think about him without being in pain. Truthfully, I didn't know how to be happy. Happiness was a department store display — a false façade behind a glass window I could never breach but only dream of. I had to learn what happiness was.

The memory of KwanYin's embrace faded, returning me to the couch in Dr. Truth's office. She had an enormous box of tissues and a glass of water ready for me. I drank the water and blew my nose, processing. Dr. Truth hummed quietly; the song might have been "Ain't No Grave."

I hadn't given up on love; I had done exactly what I needed to do. My sorrow and misery had become a poison seeping into all aspects of my life. This poison almost killed me. If anything, such suffering had been the betrayal of our love. Turning treasure into torture was a sin. From a magical perspective, my addiction to pain only pushed the possibility of being with Raven further away. As long as I was focused on his past, harbouring longing and resentment, the holographic universe returned more of the same to me. My unconscious emotional insistence upon tragedy was stronger than death in keeping us apart.

I had not abandoned my quest after all. As the dream had advised, I switched my focus. In Taoism, this principle is known as *wu-wei*, or non-doing. Sometimes the most direct path is the winding one. By not focusing on Raven, and instead focusing upon myself, I followed my quest without actively seeking it. The flowers were my awareness of my own self-worth — the pursuit of my own happiness. In the years between then and now, I found myself again. The creative pursuits of childhood

I had abandoned in the face of parental criticism were now my way of life. I had learned the price of conformity to the dominant culture and now stood firmly in the soil of my own self. I found beauty in the most mundane places — pulling out my phone and snapping photos in a Zen-like trance of immersive love for the world. I laughed; I cried. I learned to love both.

I had not been idle for twenty years; I had grown up. I worked to recover the lost child I had once been, peeling back layers of trauma with archaeological precision. I had a forever family and knew how to be part of one. I spent day after day practicing honest communication about matters of the heart, especially when it was terrifying. I was the woman I needed to become. The old me had been unable to conceive a world of love; she didn't know what love was. She had needed to learn. Along the way, I learned to face sorrow and fear.

I had spent many circles being the Warder; I knew the traditional ritual challenge by heart. I had never fully understood until now.

It is better you should fall forward onto this blade than enter the circle with fear in your heart.

Perfect love and perfect trust were concepts I had paid lip service to. Perfect love and perfect trust were about your core relationship with the Universe and yourself. Practicing magic without truly loving yourself was playing Russian roulette with a grenade; eventually your magic was going to explode in your face no matter what you did. The sad truth was you that had told the magic to do so.

Although I hadn't been aware at the time, stepping

away from our relationship and my painful perspective had been the best thing I could do. I needed to be the person who believed love was possible for me. My time away from the obsessive, ping pong pendulum swing of my bipolar relationship with our love had allowed me room to become myself and let go of all my angst.

I looked up from my reverie, struck by the lightning of insight. Deep inside, old beliefs were beginning to burn; a new and improved self rising from the ashes. Dr. Truth stopped singing, raising an eyebrow. "You satisfy your demons?"

"For now, at least." I laughed, relieved.

"Good. Now go act like it." She shooed me out of her office with a smile. She was pleased.

13

No MATTER how much conscious conviction I possessed, my subconscious mind was still not on board. If the automaton of my unconscious beliefs could not divert my attention away from the task of finding Raven, she would resort to other tried and tested means. She had a status quo to preserve, after all. I was threatening her purpose and very sense of self.

Dreaming, I found myself back at school, working on an elaborate cosplay build — an intricate, armoured chest plate. Unlike normal nerds, who opt for foam or worbla, I was using actual metal. Unfortunately, this level of metal work was outside of my skill set. Fortunately, I had some very adept friends. To my surprise, the person helping me with the build was not one of my crazy-talented cosplay friends — not Shimmer or Shade — but one of my BFA classmates.

Tucker and I had several classes together, including Figure Drawing and Installation 2. He was a tall man, strongly built in an honest country way, with a mop of ruddy curls. Art school was full of pretentious people, and the men were especially pompous. I appreciated how different Tucker was from the rest of them. Like me, he came from humble roots. His powerful installation had documented his childhood on a tobacco farm and the indelible marks — some very physical — tobacco farming had left on his family. He was also as much of a trickster as I was, reclaiming expensive school mascots from the trash and permanently installing them as impromptu works of art. The grounds and maintenance department had determined they were too expensive to remove, so they stayed, a permanent protest of the budgeting shenanigans and waste of tuition.

I was irrationally glad to see him, pleased he was helping me with my project. As we laboured over the armour, passing tools and materials back and forth, our hands often brushed in the casual way of comfortable friends. Despite the normalcy of the act, I was intimately aware of each accidental touch. Between the ease with which we worked and the awareness of contact, tension grew. In glances and bumps, we telegraphed the connection between us. I waited with baited breath, hoping something would happen.

I was easily distracted in the dream realm. Although I possessed a singular purpose, my sleeping self believed dreams were not real. Here, I could safely indulge my repressed desires and receive attention I could not when awake. I had known of my feelings for Tucker for some time, but I was also aware our window had passed. I had been half in love with him, but so myopically focused on graduating in spite of insurmountable obstacles thrown my way, I had missed how he felt about me. In keeping with his upbringing — unlike the rest of the art-school boys (and most of male modernity) — he would not push. So he never approached me in the nice guy^{tm} way. I had been too oblivious to his little acts of kindness to realize what they meant. Being with him in this space felt like a gift — an opportunity to see what we could have had, but never would.

Dream Tucker was in keeping with his corporeal self, a perfect southern gentleman. Which made perfect sense, of a sort. My waking mind reminded me of Raven several times throughout the dream. Real Tucker would never behave inappropriately either, especially not in approaching someone already in a relationship. The longer we laboured side by side, the more aware I was of my love for him. I was filled with terrible sadness and regret for never acting upon or recognizing those feelings at the time. All too soon, my chest-piece was completed. With a hug goodbye, Tucker was gone.

The sadness and the love were with me when I awoke. I was filled with irrational urges to open Instagram and apologize for never realizing how he felt about me. I wanted to ask him to make art with me, to reach out and right the missed moment of our past. I didn't. I knew it was unalterably too late. "Too late now," I quoted with a bittersweet smile. I sat with the feeling, speaking to myself in the bathroom mirror of forgiveness and acceptance, attempting to move through the guilt I felt for having thoughts of another. Even with my mindfulness, the feelings did not leave. On the contrary, they multiplied.

All day long, I was painfully aware of my own charm, oozing pheromones. When I looked at the waiter during lunch, meeting his eyes to ask if the soup of the day was gluten free, I could feel the tension between us. He was flirting with all his customers for better tips — it was a Saturday afternoon full of ladies having lunch, after all — but I could feel his rising response when we locked eyes. After he left the table, I excused myself and fled to the privacy of the bathroom to have a quick conversation with myself in the mirror. I considered my reflection for a few moments, marvelling. The purple eyeshadow I had applied to match my Wicked shirt seemed sensual and smoky, turning my eyes almost green. I saw in them the same power Raven had in his eyes — the piercing, hypnotic gaze which drew lovers in. Startled, I returned to the table and spent the rest of lunch refusing to look at the server.

After an entire day of feeling powerful while simultaneously failing at everything I tried to accomplish, I gave up. The haunting sense of guilt returned full force. I recognized the tenor of dream-induced fixation, a friendship turned into desire and deeper fondness overnight. I had mistaken this misdirection for love once before. Unlike the first planted dream desire, this one was founded in more fact than fantasy, and should have been easier for my automaton to foster. But she had not counted on my awareness. I saw the tendency to fall in love with someone else when I was making progress in my path toward Raven.

When I met my ex, I had been fully focused on self-improvement, ready and waiting for Raven. Instead, I had allowed the flim-flam man into my life, losing sight of my goal over the course of a weekend and the two months of "talking" which followed. I disgusted myself; I was no better than a cheater, betraying the man who braved the forces of the underworld to come back from the dead for me. I wallowed in self-deprecation, dressing myself down for the desires of my heart. Underneath it all, I still wanted to reach out to Tucker. I felt sick.

14

FRUSTRATED AND ANGRY AT MYSELF, I sought my sister's help and advice through the aid of a tarot reading. Sitting across from me at the large wooden kitchen table, she handed me the deck.

I loved this tarot deck with its surreal, symbolic imagery. The deck was the most honest one we owned and so I sought its help in times of trouble, even though it was never gentle with me. I was grateful the damn cards would even work for me at all, though I was a little miffed they still held a grudge after so many years. I had given them to Rhiannon in an act of contrition, which had sufficed to appease their ire enough for them to deign to speak to me. They hadn't forgiven me for leaving them behind. Abandoning them so gave them their quirky nature and uncanny power, but they were still angry and resentful toward me. They were a cursed object, altered forever by their unconventional baptism at a magical site. As I held them, my mind slipped back to the story of their making.

———

THE FIRST TIME we went to Lydia's bridge we approached it from the wrong side. The five of us — Rhiannon, Rubee, Liza, and JR and I — had gone to investigate the site based on local rumours. Parking the car in the lot of a nearby housing complex, we hiked through what had seemed like a small amount of kudzu from the road. Once immersed in the vines, however, we quickly learned why spells such as entangle were effective deterrents in D&D. What had seemed like a yard's worth of vines took us the better part of an hour to traverse.

When we finally reached our destination, we were hot and grumpy, pausing to crack open the soda bottles we carried in our pockets. Most of us paused to light cigarettes, drawing in the smoke with heavy drags. I recapped my soda and pushed through the curtain of vines obscuring the entrance. I stepped into the shade of the underpass, drawing a deep breath of air. I expected the air to be cool and welcoming; instead, it felt stale.

The interior barrel of the bridge was a riot of colours and confusion, overlapping graffiti competing for available space. Unlike the newer, more modern overpass decorated with successive layers of memorials to the dead teens of each year and requisite expressions of school spirit, this older bridge was covered in a much more aggressive display. Occult symbols of dubious nature covered the walls, marking this space as the territory of those who practiced much darker magic. A Christian would have called them Satanic. While some of these symbols were used by those who followed the Church of Satan, these particular sigils held a uniquely Christian vibration only present in those who are choosing to subvert Christian practices for an evil purpose.

I could feel and see the layers of malignancy and misery covering the structure. This space was dedicated to darkness and debauchery. I would not have been surprised to find animal bones. Trash littered the ground, evidence of multiple parties, teenage sexual exploration, and obligatory drug use. I picked my way past several piles, deeply disturbed by the display. Something near the opposite opening drew me to it magnetically, a soft call of sorrow in such a stagnant and sickening space. Pulled by the current of magic, I followed the signal only I could feel, tracing it to its origin on the outer curve of the bridge, where inside became outside, the liminal door — as it were. There, at eye level, I found the most disturbing painting yet — a depiction of Lydia herself.

Lydia was a local legend so infamous her story had been published in several books and was well known in the ghost hunting community. Waiting by the side of the road, she would flag down the cars of solitary travellers, usually men. Stranded and alone, she would beg for a ride home. Usually, she shivered with the cold. Many a gallant man would offer her his jacket, which she would accept. Upon arriving at her house, the young man would come to open her door, only to find his passenger and his jacket gone. Knocking on the door, the young man would meet his passenger's mother, who explained that her daughter was dead. As soon as he went to check, his jacket would be found hanging from her grave. The story claimed she had been stranded on her way home from prom, struck by a passing motorist and killed. Unable to return home, she haunted the scene of her death, waiting for a kind soul to take her home.

The crude painting on the wall before me did no justice to the beauty described in her tales. A primitive stick figure was depicted, a ball and chain tethered to her ankle. Below the scrawled portrait, her name was sloppily written in the same dull grey spray. Although the portrait may have been simplistic, the magic it contained was powerful. Someone had taken the ghost of a scared girl and deliberately bound her here. I stared in horror at the picture, trying to imagine the level of cruelty required for such an act. Being trapped in the afterlife, unable to move on, was traumatic enough. Binding her further, forcing her into etheric servitude, was downright evil. I stood there shaking for some moments, dimly aware of the others calling to me.

"Kara," Rhiannon asked, coming around the curved corner of the bridge until she stood beside me "What is it?"

Wordlessly, I gestured at the crude image before me, listening to her sharp intake of breath as she came to the same realizations I had. After a moment, she spoke.

"We have to fix this." Her hazel eyes narrowed as she frowned in anger.

"Definitely. We need to fix this whole place, including her. Cleanse the whole bridge." I gestured with a sweep of my arm.

"What are you thinking?" She looked around, considering.

"We're going to need a lot of paint. And holy water. And help." I shrugged slightly.

I turned to look at my sister, seeing her nod decisively, sunlight glinting off the corner of her glasses and her coppery hair. Silhouetted against the bridge, with the sunlight flowing behind her, she appeared as a Celtic Goddess, a spot of brightness against the dark where we stood.

"Let's figure out the best way back here. I don't want to carry gallons of paint through kudzu." Rhiannon turned, looking at the way we had not come, seeking a shorter route.

"Neither do I," I agreed.

We found a quicker path through the woods. A simple plasticized white fence demarcated the property line. Rhiannon and I used the top rung of the fence as a vaulting horse to propel ourselves easily over to the other side. Rubee was tall enough to stretch her long legs over the top rail. Liza and JR, lacking our gymnastic background or Rubee's height, were forced to awkwardly clamber.

We returned over the course of the next few weekends, armed with trash bags, paint, holy water, sage, and salt. Thus equipped, we proceeded to clear, clean, and ultimately cleanse the bridge. On our last day, when all else had been refreshed and readied for blessing, Rhiannon and I took two brushes and approached the binding image with our holy-water-infused paint. We painted Lydia in white, giving her wings to fly away and a long white gown to cover her ball and chain. We painted the words "You Are Free" above her new image.

I closed my eyes, sinking my awareness into the rich forest soil beneath me. I breathed in and out, pulling the vibrant green of Gaia up into my body and pushing out everything else. Once I was fully grounded, I focused my awareness on my heart chakra, centering my energy. In my mind's eye, I opened the door to the other side, seeing a bright nimbus of white light appear, brilliant beams spilling out the sides of the bridge mouth.

I focused on the image of Lydia herself, calling to her softly. "Lydia," I began in silent evocation, "hear me. You have been trapped here far too long, dear one." I focused on the image of the girl we had found in the old school records, calling to her.

"Goddess, hear me. Your child is lost. Come help her find her way."

A brilliant burst of birdsong filled the air, along with the scent of flowers. Serenity wafted toward me on the beams of otherworldly light, and I choked back tearful sobs as I saw Lydia take on a mist-like form as she approached the door, bliss and happiness written on her face. She stepped through and the light vanished, leaving only a faint hint of magic in the air. I surreptitiously wiped away a tear with the back of my hand, taking a deep breath.

"Now that's done, I need a cigarette," Rhiannon said. Tobacco smoke is purifying, after all. She pulled out her silver Zippo and a box of Newport 100s, their bright turquoise stark in the mid-afternoon shadows under the trees. At the sound of her lighter flipping closed, I could hear the others making their way toward us.

Several hours later, after dinner and preparations, we returned to the bridge, three extra people in tow. Buoyed by my earlier success, I enjoyed the excitement of participating in a ritual with so many people. Usually, there were only four of us — Rubee, Liza, Rhiannon, and me — one for each element. Tonight, we had enough for a double circle, had any of the other four the experience to successfully call the quarters. Five more and we would be a full thirteen. We were over halfway there. I was pleased with the size of our group — a rare accomplishment amongst adults, let alone teenagers.

Laughing and talking, we walked the short distance through the woods and began setting up our circle. We laid a fire in the pit we had cleaned, and Rhiannon and I set about inscribing a circle into the dirt floor of the underpass. JR was busy being uncomfortable, having brought his girlfriend Karen along. Liza was busy pouting and trying to get JR's attention. Phyllis was talking with her boyfriend — neither of whom had any experience in ritual. Rubee helped with the fire, since it was her element, but she didn't have the knowledge or experience to be of much help with the rest of the preparations. Normally, Rhiannon and I would have been giving each other looks, communing in our silent way how annoyed we were to do all the work. Tonight, we were too excited to care. We had given them each small tasks appropriate to their level, and there was a certain pleasure in being deferred to.

Finally, the circle was ready. We four entered first, accepting the ritual challenge and receiving our five-fold kisses and blessings. Anointed and oiled, we stood at our accustomed places, waiting to receive the others. One by one, they approached the circle to be challenged by Rubee. She enjoyed the role of Warder, pleasure sparkling in her dark eyes as she held the ritual knife and spoke the words of testing. When she had finished, I stepped behind her to close the circle.

Our circle thus closed, we called the elements.

"Hail, Spirits of the East, Bringers of the Dawn, keepers of the mind," I intoned, closing my eyes. I reached into the ether and pulled, calling wind toward me, seeing it sweep around our circle, enclosing us all in pale blue light. Using my wand, I inscribed a pentacle in the east, sealing the bridge I had opened Between the Worlds.

Rubee continued, followed by Rhiannon, ending with Liza's call. I watched the elements arrive, rising around our circle and ringing them in light. I enjoyed seeing the swirls of the colours, feeling and hearing the taste of each element as they joined our circle. Rhiannon stepped into the centre, as close as she could to the fire, drawing the energy up into the sky, down into the ground, and sealing it, leaving us encased in a softly glowing sphere.

The innermost layer was a mosaic of playful swirls and eddies, twirling pastel tones combining and recombining in an endless variation of shapes. Beyond, a sphere of fire danced, fierce flames licking at the wind. Outside the fire, a gentle mist rose, coalescing into raindrops which ran down the sphere in waterfalls to pool in streams and rise as mist once more in an endless cycle of evaporation and precipitation. The outermost layer was formed from a chaotic riot of vines, twining shapes encasing us inside a living ball. I knew only Rhiannon and I could see our circle, and I felt momentarily sad for the others. I could not imagine how blind I would feel without my Sight, or how much I would miss the simple beauty of magic.

Rhiannon's voice startled me out of my reverie, calling my attention back to the present. She was in High Priestess mode, her carriage erect and upright. Her voice was clear and rung with command. "The Circle is cast and we are Between the Worlds."

What she said was true; I saw the world behind our sheltered sphere shift subtly and take on an otherworldly tone. Anything was possible in this space. I shivered slightly, goosebumps drawing down my skin.

We had completed the words of intent but had yet to begin any invocations or evocations when I felt something amiss. A prickling sensation rose on the back of my neck; I was certain we were being watched. I resisted the urge to turn and confront our observer, knowing that doing so would only spook the others.

Rhiannon sat across from me, continuing to speak. Surely, if something did stand behind me, her face would show it. Instead, she wore the perfect picture of priestessly calm.

In spite of what my rational mind told me, I could feel a sort of darkness gathering beyond the confines of the circle. In a perfect world, the compass would have aligned perfectly to the old road, letting us line up our quarters with the entrances to the tunnel. Instead, we sat diagonally, so that the openings to the bridge lay behind our untrained guests, none of whom possessed the Sight. I stared out into the darkness beyond the bridge, angled to see a sliver of forest which led to the stream.

Beyond the stream lay an unknown landscape, presumably part of the ancient plantation — which was now simply a stately gentleman's farm — the sort which boasted beautiful colonial-revival architecture and white rail fences around the house, a mask of casual southern opulence which belied the dark past.

I knew too much about this town and her history to be fooled. I had spent many of my childhood afternoons sitting at the piano, listening to the tales of the older generations. Whatever this land had been before it was purchased after The War, it was not part of the Quaker section of town. Most of *that* was under water. According to legend, when Jacob Dale bought the property in 1866, it already held a large, if uncultured, house. Given the timing of the purchase and other local lore about the long-standing dispute between the

Mendenhalls and their non-Quaker neighbours, I had my own theories about the history of this land.

This particular section of the property possessed a distinct malevolence I felt in the marrow of my bones; a cold enmity waiting to devour me. *I wonder what recorded memories these rocks hold to disturb me so much. Then again, I probably don't want to know.* No-one else seemed bothered by parts of these woods the way I was, but they wouldn't be. The primary privilege of the White South is their powerful denial, the ability to pretend away a past they would prefer to ignore. I, on the other hand, had never been blessed with such forgetfulness. My minimal melanin might allow me to pass unmolested among the living, but not among the dead. The law of the land in which they lived considered me property, no matter how light I appeared. The entire South was a living nightmare for me, a place I could never quite relax. I never knew when the past would literally come back to haunt me.

There's nothing out there waiting in the darkness watching you. It's nothing. Focus on the ritual. No matter what might wait beyond, a creature of evil could not cross the stream unaided. Such a being also could not violate the sacred space of the bridge or pass beyond the absolute boundaries of our protective circle. So long as I stayed within the circle, I would be safe. Despite my intent to be present and enjoy the ritual I had been so excited to be a part of, my unease continued to rise.

In the midst of my growing tension, during which time seemed to crawl, the world erupted into chaos. A mix of cacophonous calls rang through the woods, accompanied by the sound of small cylinder engines, which could have been anything from chainsaws to dirt bikes and four wheelers. Bouncing lights appeared in the woods behind the bridge, beams crisscrossing in the dark as though a large search party bore down upon us. My ears thought they heard braying hounds, but the moment passed, an echo of the past, perhaps. All around me, the untrained panicked.

Under the chaos, I could hear Rhiannon's voice of command urging everyone to stay calm and inside the circle. We were safe inside. Spiritual adversaries could do us no harm. Physical ones had a group of eight to face, several of whom were capable in a fight. Legally, we were on no-man's land, a strip owned by the railroad. Only they had the right to call the authorities and have us removed. Their business hours were long over and pressing charges to have us removed by the authorities was outside the pay grade of whoever would be on call. The sheriff himself could only tell us to go home. We knew how things worked in this town. The sheriff's niece was in our French class, after all. Rubee, Rhiannon, and I all also knew how said niece acquired her A from our French teacher. It wasn't her pronunciation skills.

But teenagers are teenagers and never listen to reason. Unnerved by the disturbing din approaching through the darkness, they deserted us. As soon as the first one broke the boundary in their flight, the energy bubble around us burst, my safety net shattered beyond repair. Left alone, Rhiannon and I stared at each other and swore under our breaths for the briefest of seconds before springing into action.

We doused the candles and fire, throwing implements and tools into our book bags with alacrity. *Where did Rubee go? What the fuck? Some badass she is to turn and run at the first sign of trouble.* Rubee sprinted back into the bridge, throwing knives in hand. *Oh right, her new knives. She must have gone to get them.* Rubee quickly joined us in the cleanup efforts. Finally, our last item was retrieved.

Together we raced for the car. I could feel our pursuers behind us, both those of the flesh and those of the spirit. I sensed the presence of dogs; this time I smelled them. Motivated by the desire to avoid even an ephemeral dog bite, I vaulted over the fence, flinging myself over as quickly as I could. Focused on fleeing, I did not hear the soft thud of something hitting the ground behind me. Only later, when I arrived home, would I find my tarot deck missing. Unfortunately, it rained that night. Although we retrieved them the next day, the cards have never forgiven me.

15

RETURNING TO THE PRESENT, I reminded myself that
focusing on the story of the cards would not benefit my
reading in any way. I pushed the past from my mind,
bringing my awareness to focus on my uncomfortable
present. My guilt returned with full force and I chan-
nelled the feeling into my hands, feeding the cards
images related to my query. *What do I need to know about
this?* I asked them. *Why do I feel this way, what should I do?*
I shuffled the deck sideways in my hands — the cards
were too large for conventional shuffling. Nor would
they appreciate such an act. Something clicked. Satisfied, I stopped shuffling and handed the deck to my
sister.

I watched her lay out the cards in an arch, their blue
ocean-space backs as beautiful as they had always been,
albeit much more worn around the edges. White specks
dotted their surface, small spaces where the substrate
had sloughed off with use. She began the reading,

turning one large, rounded rectangle over with her long cameo fingers, the doorway in the centre of the arch — the general overview or theme of the reading. The Star: a pale white woman with a short pixie cut depicted in profile, gazing off to the left, into the past. The light of insight kissed her crown, granting her guidance and intuition.

Rhiannon looked at me, raising her thick eyebrows in an unspoken question. *Do I need to explain?* I shook my head no. She proceeded to the next.

She flipped the next card, the foundation of the right side of the arch — the past. This card was the two of disks: Change. She looked at me again questioningly, and once more I shook my head. Directly above the past lay the card for the present. Rhiannon flipped it over to reveal the ten of wands: Oppression. A small, pale human figure stood in a stone box, his back to the viewer. Ten bolts of energy shot down toward the stone cell. Although I understood the general meaning, I could not comprehend its current context.

I looked at Rhiannon, furrowing my brow in confusion. Interpreting my nonverbal communication accurately, she added a secondary card from the leftover deck. The nine of swords: Cruelty. A tearful eye, heavily made up, dominated the centre of the card. Blood dripped from gashes on the cheekbone, spilling toward barbed wire which blocked the face. Combined with the first card, the meaning was clear. I was the victim of self-imposed suffering, trapped by my own self. I nodded and Rhiannon continued.

The third card on the right of the arch was hidden

influences. Rhiannon flipped it over, revealing the Moon — the card of dreams and illusions. Of course illusions would be hidden influences. I made a nonverbal noise of frustration and she drew another card for clarification: the Queen of Swords. A blonde woman hid in the background of the card, multiple masks obscuring her face. I picked up the card to look at it more closely and read the small hints of script written there. *Rational, logical, objective*, the script read. I considered this unusual pairing: illusions and the masks of rationality. I nodded, encouraging her to proceed.

At the top of the arch sat the keystone card, the one which represented obstacles in my path. Rhiannon flipped it over, revealing the Princess of Swords; the card we both equated with me. A woman stared distrustfully from its surface, her dark hair coloured red from blood. A crown of eyes graced her head. In her right arm, she clutched a sword and some broken chains. This card meant I was standing in my own way, but I did not understand how. I nodded again; I needed the rest of the reading before the meanings would be completely clear. Each card was a spice in the seasoning of meaning, adding their flavours together collectively and influencing the overall aroma and taste. Taken separately, they informed, but could also be misleading. After all, basil could be both savoury and sweet, depending on the other spices it was paired with.

Past the keystone, the arch turned to the left, the next card informing how someone else feels in the situation. The Devil needed no explanation, but I was at a loss to understand who it represented. I raised my eyebrows in question and Rhiannon topped The Devil with another card: the eight of swords — Interference. Two half-naked women — both with generic white-girl peach skin— towered over a road that split past them. Between them, a figure huddled on a bench, over-whelmed and distraught by the weight of making a decision. I examined the script on this card as well, seeking more context clues: *anguish of too much introspection* and *lack of perseverance*. The Devil was me, or at least part of my psyche.

Past the keystone came the final three cards of the arch — the recommended course of action and the possible outcomes of following (or not) the advice given. Rhiannon flipped over the card for advice, revealing the nine of wands: Strength. A stone block, much like the cell on the ten of wands, filled the image as it was exploding from within, a brilliant light shat-tering its sides into multiple small pieces. The message seemed clear: destroy the cage which contains you. Still, I wanted to be certain. I gave her the look once more and she added another clarifying card. The seven of wands: Valor. Two cliffs dominated the card and a lone figure leapt the chasm between them. I nodded, knowing the cards would not be more specific than this.

The two outcomes at the base of the arch could not have been starker in their difference. On one hand, if I followed the advice, sat the nine of cups: Happiness. A bright swirl of light was surrounded by a collection of images which always reminded me very much of a quilt. On the other hand, if I failed to heed the wisdom of the cards, sat the seven of cups: Indolence. A wilting flower stood alone in a wasteland, bare cracked desert spreading to the horizon. Empty cups littered the land-scape while a dark sky hovered ominously above. I frowned. Rhiannon added two more cards — one clari-fier for each. On top of Happiness she placed the Knight of Cups: the card I associated with Raven. On it, was the profile of a man facing the left, the colours inverted so his light skin and dark hair had become blue skin and white hair. A single red rose sat in front of his face. I knew the words on this card by heart: *ability to give, devotion to a loved person, spiritual relationship, the family of one's choice*. On top of Indolence she placed the seven of disks: Failure. A small, sad figure slumped helplessly, heavy dark disks hovering overhead.

I sat silently for some time, considering the cards in context with each other. Rhiannon too sat quietly, allowing me space to process. I returned to the right of the arch, reading the cards in order. In the past: change. In the present: self-inflicted torture. The hidden influ-ences were the illusion of rationality, and the tendency to wear masks and hide the truth. The obstacle was myself. How another person felt was another part of me — determined to cause temptation and interference. I was advised to break free of my cell and strive for the impossible. If I did, I would find happiness and Raven. If I did not, disaster and failure awaited.

Finally, I spoke. "I think I understand, but do not *know.*" I emphasized the word to make my meaning clear. "The issue arises in my mind. I know this. But what does this mean? Why?"

"Your mind seeks the comfort of the known and the

normal. When your automatic responses are threatened, they reach for the familiar. You know this. Your mind is threatened by the possibility of Raven, so your monkey brain distracts you by trying to foster fixations on others."

"So it runs from love by pursuing love?" This made little sense.

"Was love ever safe for you in childhood?" She already knew the answer. I did too, but she had a point.

"No. But I still don't understand."

Rhiannon paused for a moment, choosing her words carefully before proceeding. "What you're experiencing is perfectly normal. I told you, when Bevan and I first got together, I was so scared of true intimacy, I was shaking. I was so scared I allowed a bunch of stupid stuff to cloud my judgement and then became fixated on Dick, who was exactly like every other man I had dated before. I'm not saying Tucker would have been at all like David or any of the guys before him, but your mind reached for anyone it could distract you with."

"But I feel so guilty. I don't like seeing myself this way." I raised my shoulders in a defensive shrug, shrinking my neck as I lowered my head.

"What way? As human? You just figured out this lesson and instead of acting on the impulse, you are already questioning it. Maybe instead of belittling yourself for being human, you should praise yourself for growing so quickly. Obstacles are going to happen. It's how you handle them that counts. Why are you always so hard on yourself?" Her stare was as direct as her tone, her hazel eyes boring into my soul.

"Because I have to be perfect. I have to be good enough." I threw my arms up in helpless resignation.

"You always say that about Raven. Why do you think you're not good enough?" She cocked her head to the side and considered me.

"Because I feel like I don't deserve him." *How could I?*

"Why is that?"

"Because I was never allowed to have any of the things I wanted in childhood. I was told I didn't deserve them because I didn't take care of my things."

"Children never take care of their things," she laughed, no doubt thinking of her daughter. "That's how children are. Your parents couldn't afford to buy you the things you wanted, but instead of being honest, they blamed it on you. My parents were poor too, and it was awful. I never knew if there would be food, or when the power would go out. But I had plenty of toys, and new clothes every year. I had a support system of extended family who provided for me. Your parents denied you that. You had a childhood of extreme deprivation, and I don't think you realize it."

I knew she was right. I couldn't imagine getting new clothes every year, not even now. My clothing had come from yard sales, my toys from the trash. I had eaten food deemed unfit for human consumption, and once, even maggots. I was crying. I removed my glasses to wipe the tears away with the hem of my flannel shirt. A red thread dangled there.

"So, on an unconscious level, I don't feel I deserve him because he is my heart's desire. And every other heart's desire was denied me because of my supposed unworthiness. So my mind seeks to sabotage the relationship and damage it, thereby proving I didn't deserve it."

Rhiannon nodded.

"Damn, that's messed up." I subconsciously sabotaged and destroyed the very things I wanted most so I could feel secure in my story of unworthiness. "Just like with the cards." The light of *satori* dawned in my mind, shedding light in dark spaces, illuminating long forgotten corners of my mind. I imagined I was the Star — the spark of awareness gracing my crown.

"In what way?" Rhiannon waited for me to explain.

"The moment I saw this deck, I fell in love with it. I went back multiple times to purchase them, saving money so they could be mine. And then I had them for what, two weeks before the incident at the bridge happened? I believed I didn't deserve them for leaving them behind. So I had to give them to you, not because the cards demanded it, but because it was the only way I could believe they would work for me again."

"Yes. That's incredibly insightful."

I stared at the cards, a bittersweet sorrow filling my heart. Of all the decks I had tried, none — other than these — had ever worked for me. I had long since stopped trying to have a tarot deck, contenting myself with oracle cards instead. I understood. As painful and sad as it was for me to give up such a tool, abandoning Raven would feel far worse. I closed my eyes, thanking the cards for their powerful lesson. I would not let my "unworthiness" stop me again.

16

I FOUND myself on a university campus, walking with Thor along a cement walkway between buildings. I had no memory of how we arrived here, wherever here was. I studied my surroundings, searching for clues. Although it felt like a warm spring day, the foliage was the darker green of summer. I was in one of the other realms: perhaps a dream realm or a section of the astral.

I was glad to be walking with a trusted and competent friend, since I did not know why we were here or where we were headed. Backup is always a good plan, and Thor was among the few people I trusted to guard my back. One of my oldest friends, we first bonded during our shared past in the same gaming clan. In an environment dominated by white men and structured around Alpha male dominance games inherent to toxic masculinity, we were statistical outliers: minorities traditionally excluded from the clubhouse for their perceived inferiority. Determined to prove ourselves equal, we overachieved and over-dominated, pushing our badassery to the pinnacle until we were feared by the rest of the clan.

We honed our teamwork and communication skills during countless battles until we were banned from playing together in clan games. Time spent side by side focusing on a common goal strengthened our psychic connections, plugging us into the neural network our gaming group referred to as "the brain LAN." Our connection speed was so high it convinced even the most skeptical members among the group; they were the ones who coined the term. Long after I had outgrown my association with the rest of the team, Thor was still one of my favourite people. In addition to our camaraderie, Thor had a military background and magical training of his own. He was a solid partner to pick for any fight. His presence here reassured me.

As we rounded the corner of the building, the rear of another came into view. Although a small copse of pine trees separated the two structures, I could clearly see the back patio and picnic tables sitting behind the second. A lone figure sat facing the doors of the building, eating his lunch.

The set of his shoulders struck me as familiar — the effortless ease with which he maintained a relaxed, yet perfect posture where another would have slouched. My heart quickened, its transmission slipping gears as it accelerated quickly. *Could it be Raven?* An older black gentleman dressed in standard issue professorial garb — white button-down shirt and tie, sweater, slacks —

exited the building, stopping to speak with the man eating lunch.

"Afternoon, Raven!" the professor hailed. I nearly jumped with excitement. *It was him! Now what?* I thought, my mind racing to catch up with my turbo-charged heart.

"Sorry, I don't have much time to talk with you right now, professor. I want to finish my lunch before I'm needed at the reference desk." *When would that be?* "It's almost 2:30 now." The phrasing of his answer seemed slightly odd, as if it were more addressed to me and my unspoken question than a response to the professor. *Fantastic.* Now, I only had to find the library and its reference desk. I turned, seeking my bearings.

"What's up, Starsister?" Thor asked playfully, giving me "the look." "You're light years away."

I turned to face him, feeling a little guilty. He was right; I had been ignoring him since entering this strange space. If anyone would understand, he would. I smiled and met his warm walnut eyes. "I'm sorry, Star-brother. I thought I recognized someone I know. And, in fact, I did." I paused, searching for the right words, and settled on the simplest. "I have to go see a guy about a thing. Because... synchronicity." I smiled sheepishly, shrugging my shoulders at my inability to articulate more clearly.

He grinned at my reference to our gaming tactics, recognizing our old code phrase for solo reconnaissance missions. His expressive smile spoke of understanding without saying a word, the tawny skin around his eyes crinkling with amusement. One of my favourite things about our relationship was that it was built on a rapport bordering on telepathy and required no explanations. True, he'd most likely tease me about this later, but I could accept such a thing. After all, had our roles been reversed, I would have done the same. He ruffled my long hair with one hand.

"Go get your guy. You got this, yo!" He gave me an encouraging wink, his brown eyes twinkling with amusement.

I threw my arms around him in a quick hug. "Thank you, Thor."

"You can thank me by going to talk to him. Go," he said, shooing me away with both hands. I grinned self-consciously and headed for the library.

Unlike most libraries, which greet patrons upon entrance with a desk or community area, this library began without preamble — one entered directly into the stacks. Curious, I glanced at the titles while also scanning for Raven. I wandered the aisles distractedly, seeking him, but also intrigued by the books. I've always loved libraries — one part temple of knowledge and one part TARDIS, capable of transporting the reader anywhere. Urgent as my desire to find Raven was, I had to indulge my bibliophilic curiosity. The first entire section of the stacks was filled with blank books, volume after volume of empty journals with varying covers set on display under lights. The last three aisles were much the same. *What kind of library is this?*

I exited an aisle, turning left only to collide with someone I hadn't seen coming. They caught me, steadying me before I could fall. A nanosecond stretched to infinity in my mind as I was aware of the rapid electrical response occurring in my nervous system. Familiar currents of energy raced toward my brain in tingling waves, sending goosebumps down my spine. My body knew what was happening before my mind. Struggling to process the sudden flood of sensory input surging through my system, I looked up into the face of my saviour. It was Raven 2.0.

He was breathtakingly beautiful. If I looked for them the echoes of his old face remained, but his face was also entirely new. His sharply sculpted lines and angles had been softened, worn down to rounder features with the deft touch of a master. If I had thought him attractive before, he was nearly angelic now; elven in his otherworldly perfection. I stared up into his bright amber eyes, focusing on him until the world narrowed to nothing but his flawless face.

"Are you ok?" he asked in a librarian's quiet, clear voice.

A shiver ran down my spine in electric waves, the current sparking small fires on my skin. *What do I say?* My racing brain began careening out of control around hair-pin curves. *Oh shit, does he recognize me? Does he even know me? Frak frak frak. Stay cool, Riordan. Stay cool. You can't stay in his arms forever, girl. You've got to speak up.* I struggled to regain control of my mental wheel.

"I'm sorry, that was so clumsy of me. My blood sugar must be low — I haven't eaten any lunch." I rambled awkwardly, desperately trying to inject levity into my tone and failing miserably. *Low blood sugar? Seriously? You sound like an idiot.* As many times as I had imagined this moment, my fantasies never involved falling into his arms dramatically like a damsel in distress. *So much for making a good first impression and dazzling him with your sparkling wit. Frak.*

"In that case, you should probably go eat. You might want a jacket. It's about to rain out there." He smiled, nodding toward the window and the clouds gathering outside.

"That's not necessary but thank you." *This conversation is going nowhere fast. You've waited twenty years for this moment and all you can talk about is low blood sugar and the weather? Really!? You should take advantage of this moment and kiss him already.* I briefly imagined the thrill of his kiss, our unrestrained passion peaking, life imitating a bawdy romance novel. My hormones were in favour of this plan, my pulse racing as heat grew in my belly.

The rational part of my brain counselled restraint, however. *C'mon, Riordan. This is the really real world. You're not the heroine in a romance novel. You don't know whether he even recognizes you. Kissing him without consent is morally wrong, legally assault, and uncomfortably close to the salacious, exotic gypsy stereotype. This is not a bodice ripper. Damnit, say something, anything. Ask him out on a date. What if he turns me down? I don't know if I can do this!*

My nerves agreed — making the first move early in the game was too bold a move, even for me. I struggled with my desire to speak with him and the conflicting need to maintain social mores. *Maybe I should ask for his help? No, too much of a trope. You've already fallen into his arms. You don't need to appear any more helpless than you already have. You're not a wilting flower; you're a badass. Act like it. Well, what then? DO* **something**!

Before I could choose a course of action, a timid young assistant approached us. Anxiety was written all over his narrow features, his copper forehead drawn down until his jet-black brows formed a single heavy line. *Oh shit, awkward!* I quickly stepped out of Raven's arms, righting my clothing self-consciously.

"Excuse me, Raven. I'm sorry to interrupt, but we need your help at the desk...?" Timid Young Assistant asked, his voice pitched high toward the end of his question, looking uncomfortable. I could imagine exactly how the scene looked from his perspective. Sadly, it wasn't what it looked like at all, no matter how desperately I wanted it to be. Even if I had entertained a very brief bodice-ripping scenario in my head while he held me, something else was happening here. *Damnit.*

I smiled and gestured for them to go ahead. If he worked here and was returning from his lunch break, he wasn't going anywhere for a while. In the meantime, I would figure out what to say to him. *"Do you remember me?" I was on a runaway train headed straight into crazy town with such a line. "I've been looking for you?" No, too cheesy. "Do I know you?" Also trite. I might as well ask him if he came here often or fell from heaven. Maybe the library has a book?* I chuckled, imagining such a resource shelved some-where in the self-help section. *Sure. "How to Talk to Your Soulmate When He Doesn't Know You" would be shelved right between "Awkward Pickup Lines for Women Over Thirty" and "How to Tell If You're Delusional."*

I wandered into another section of the library,

agonizing over what I could say. This area apparently housed the comic book collection. *What kind of library is this?* I wandered through the stacks, searching for my favourite titles. They were all on display. *How convenient.* After the comics was a section of sci-fi collectibles, including some incredibly realistic looking toys. *Cosplay props perhaps? How odd.*

"Curiouser and curiouser, said Alice," I muttered under my breath. I went back through the comics. They were entirely too familiar for reason. The library boasted large sections of X-Men and Wonder Woman, SuperGirl, Peggy Carter, Sailor Moon, AVP, The Crow... not a single title I had never heard of; my favourites made up the bulk of the collection. *Wait, where am I?* I had to find out.

I spun around, seeking Raven and fell into him, again. *Really?! I seriously need to get new dice if I'm going to keep botching my Dex roles.* This falling shit was getting old, especially when it ended with him catching me. I felt like a terrible romance trope. Next, my hair would be blowing in the wind as my bodice was artfully ripped to reveal the top of a shoulder and the curve of a breast. *Ugggh. Where am I?! And are those gaming books over there?* My mind spun, desperately struggling to make sense of my strange surroundings.

"Uh... hi." I giggled, blushing. *Smooth, Riordan, smooth. You sound like Princess Anna of Arendell. Now you're falling like a schoolgirl AND giggling. Frak.* This was not going as I had imagined, at all.

"Hi," he said, his brown eyes laughing. *He was laughing at me.* I couldn't find the focus to care. I was too busy babbling excitedly in my head. "Would you like to go get some lunch with me?"

I didn't care that he had already eaten. I would have said yes to anything he asked me. I was too relieved and excited. I had found him. Sixteen years of chasing him in dreams and I had finally found him. He was here, holding me. I was going to cry.

"Please." I smiled, choking back tears.

Hand in hand, we walked toward the reference desk. Timid Young Assistant was there, as was his work partner, Serious Girl.

"I'm taking the rest of the afternoon off." Raven didn't offer any explanation and they didn't ask for one. *Definitely the boss*.

"What do you want us to work on while you're gone?" Serious Girl asked, pushing her glasses further up her nose with one tawny finger.

"Work on the audio tapes," he said, donning a flannel shirt. A stray crimson thread dangled from his sleeve.

I walked, holding his hand, my head on his right shoulder. He was the perfect height. Outside, rain had begun to fall. We reached a sheltered section of pathway and he stopped, turning to face me. I stepped into his arms, looking up into his face with a happy, almost drunk grin. He tucked a stray strand of hair behind my ear, ending with his hand under my chin, holding my face like a rare flower.

"Kara, it's me." Somehow, the confession sounded neither crazy nor silly when *he* said it.

"I know." I stood in his embrace, beaming like a fool, staring up into his eyes.

"May I?"

"Please." My entire awareness centered on the nerves in my lips as we kissed, warm-cool energy rippling over the top of my head and cascading in waves down my spine, sending delicious goosebumps spreading over my skin. At first tentative and gentle, our kiss deepened with the intensity of relief. "I missed you," it said.

We stood blissfully oblivious to the rain falling all around us, kissing and crying and laughing and crying more. Eventually, he insisted we go get something to eat.

Wherever we were, there were still diners. I ordered an omelette and a salad, trusting my usual diner fare to be safe for me to eat no matter where I was. I don't remember how the food I devoured tasted; I was more focused on the feeling of his shoulder beneath my cheek, the solid weight of him. I was memorizing every detail.

People carry their residual self-image with themselves into the ether. It's somewhat idealized, but no more than social media snapshots. The astral body is much more real than anything Photoshop could produce. This was the most truthful representation of his new body I could possibly ask for. I knew I would never be able to draw him accurately enough to satisfy myself, but I could use my eidetic memory to photograph him so I would recognize him anywhere.

"What were you doing in the library?" he asked between bites of a sandwich.

"It's a library. Like I need a reason to be in one?" I joked, turning my head to give him my best Rock impression, complete with The People's Eyebrow. He'd known me long enough to know about me and books.

He grinned guiltily and we laughed together.

We left the diner for a place I assumed to be his house. The space and its décor looked like him: shabby chic furnishings, Asian scarves draped carelessly around the edges, folding screens here and there. It was minimalist and romantic in its carefree way. I'd like to say we had a deep, meaningful conversation, but such a statement would have been a lie; it would have also required the patience of saints.

———

"RAVEN?" I asked, sometime later, my head cushioned on his chest.

"Mm?" he murmured contentedly. His response sounded more draconic than human: part acknowledgement, part dragon's purr. I loved the way his contented voice rumbled in his chest.

"Why did you fall in love with me?" I rolled onto my side, propping myself up on one elbow, studying his face.

"What do you mean, love?" He shifted sleepily to face me.

"I mean the night I summoned your spirit and was going to ask you to teach me. I was an insufferably self-absorbed, angst-ridden teenage mess. What in the world did you see that inspired you to kiss me, much less fall in love with me?"

"Wow," he laughed, shaking his head. "You really don't know, do you?"

I gave him The People's Eyebrow again. It didn't work. He was laughing harder now, to the point of tears. I narrowed my eyes in mock annoyance and scowled at him.

He took a deep breath and smiled, wiping away the tears. When he spoke again, he was still chuckling under his breath and shaking his head. "Kara, my love, it boggles my mind how you can love me so much and yourself so little. You do realize we're essentially the same, you and I?"

"What do you mean?" His statement didn't tell me anything. Damn Taoists and their obtuse answers.

Now he gave me "the look." "You thought what... you were some tragically broken ugly duckling who was damaged beyond repair? And you thought I was... what, some kind of hero, a wise *sifu* come to save you?" He turned his head to the side, raising a perfect eyebrow.

"Not exactly..." I argued, trailing off, trying to avoid admitting how close he had come to the mark.

"Enlighten me, then," He sat up in the bed, crossing his legs under the sheet, and stared at me, waiting. I tried my best not to be distracted by the sight of his muscles.

"Fine. You're right. I had a Loathly Lady meets *Karate Kid* fantasy going on. My conscious thought at the time was you were a wise *sifu*. It was entirely orientalist of me and I turned you into the exotic other. In my defence, this was based upon *your* behaviour. You spent your last days on earth waxing philosophic about the Zen practice of appreciating life. It came across as pretty damn prescient. What else was I supposed to think?" I raised my right hand and opened up my palm in question, gesturing emphatically at the air.

"I can see that. But Kara, when you study martial arts, you learn things about yourself. That awareness can seem to convey a certain spiritual sense. But that attentiveness is also no different than the knowledge you now have as well. It's not some magical secret. It's mastery of the self and mindfulness in the present moment; nothing more, nothing less." He shook his head and sighed. "I'm not a wise *sifu*, just another student of The Way."

I laughed and rolled my eyes. "I'm going to tactfully refrain from mentioning that Yoda himself claimed not to be a Jedi master. True masters always claim to be students, love. You're proving my point." I stuck my tongue out at him and looked down to study a crimson thread woven through the sheets.

He laughed, a deep throaty chuckle, the sound causing champagne bubbles of happiness to rise and burst in my heart. "If that's tactful, I look forward to your blunt honesty. You said your 'conscious' thought. What was your unconscious reasoning?"

I looked back up to meet his eyes. "That's where the hero part comes in."

"Ok…" Raven cocked his head to the side, frowning slightly.

"As much as I would have fought and died on the hill of being a self-rescuing princess, I needed someone to save me. And you were the perfect person to do so."

"How so?"

"You were beautiful and deadly. My introduction to your acting career was as an avenging angel fighting for love. And you stood by your character's choices, claiming your moral compass was aligned with his decision to kill rapists and murderers. I knew you would both understand my need for vengeance towards my parents and possess a desire to kill them yourself. And most importantly — you could."

I took a deep breath and let it out slowly before continuing. "My childhood was a nightmare. My birth mother is a narcissist incapable of love. Her only motivation is the desire to have power over another human being. My birth father is a paedophile and a registered sex offender; he was the one who loved me and used my need for love as a tool to groom me. They both derived sick satisfaction from trying to break my will with as much violence as necessary. I've spent my entire life in their shadow, waiting for them to attack me again. When I'm with you, the constant, quiet panic is gone."

Raven growled and closed his eyes, taking a deep breath before opening them again. "Ok, you're right. I want to kill them. Where do they live?"

I laughed, reaching over to poke his knee with my hand. "See, hero. I was right."

He laughed, shaking his head. "Almost."

"Almost?" I raised my eyebrows.

"Almost. Your perception of me might be more accurate than I want to admit, but your assessment of yourself is still incredibly flawed."

I shrugged. "It is known."

He laughed again, running his hand through his hair. "You asked me what I saw. Suffice it to say, spirits can see the essence of the living. And what I saw in you made me fall in love. You are the strongest person I have ever known — I am in awe of your stubborn, wilful perseverance in the face of adversity."

"What you see as strength is nothing more than defiance I honed at their hands, an Arya level desire to achieve my revenge." I frowned and shook my head.

Raven laughed. "Exactly. Your response to trauma and chaos is to stand up and scream at the void in defiance. Your dogged persistence of growth through massive amounts of cognitive dissonance makes me fall in love with you again and again. I don't know many people like you. Most people are unwilling to pursue anything other than what they already know. But you..." he continued earnestly, his eyes glowing with affection, "you embrace change like a force of nature. You are a Goddess with an unconquerable will. How could I not fall in love with you?

"I was a cocky pretty boy, used to charming my way through trouble. When you looked at me with an expression of awe, I would have done almost anything to keep you. Most of the wisdom you attribute to me, you expected, and I did my best to rise to the occasion. You loved me with a fervour akin to worship. I couldn't bear to let you down; if I did, you might realize I was only an abandoned little boy, lost and broken beyond repair," he confessed, his voice cracking with vulnerability.

I laughed, crying a little at the same time. We were perfect for each other, right down to our neuroses. We had each seen the other as a superhuman force to be idolized while fearing the other would discover the truth of our brokenness. We were abandoned children grandstanding to hide our desperate need for love.

"So... we're both lost ducklings but you're the pretty one?" I raised my arched eyebrows as close to my hairline as they could reach, wrinkling my high forehead with the effort.

He tackled me, pretending to growl. "That's not what I meant." He wrapped his arms around me in a tight embrace, pulling me close to his chest. "You're the sexiest woman I've ever met. But I couldn't lead with that."

"Uhuh, sure. You're gonna have to be a whole lot more convincing, Romeo." I looked up at him playfully, daring him to act.

"Challenge accepted. May I?" His voice was suddenly deeper, sending shivers of delight down my spine. The intensity in his eyes was hypnotizing.

"Please?"

———

SOMETIME LATER I lay half on my side, head pillowed in his chest, listening to the sound of his heartbeat. One of my legs was draped over his and I luxuriated in the feeling of his chest rising and falling with each breath. One of his hands idly stroked my skin in a gentle repetitive motion, petting me. I savoured the sensation, deliberately etching all the details of the experience into my memory: the weight of his arm wrapping around me, the feeling of his skin pressing against mine, the perfect way we fit together.

In a particularly poignant moment of insight, I recognized this awareness as one of the more profoundly beautiful side effects of our peculiar relationship. Because I never knew when I would see him again, every single moment was precious. In his presence, mindfulness became an effortless way of life, a deliberate choice to live in each heartbeat and love it fully. An expansive paroxysm arose in my chest as my heart broke open; pouring out glorious; bloody; loving warmth which seeped into every cell of my being. I only realized I was joy-weeping when he spoke.

"What are you feeling, love?"

I smiled and buried my face further in his chest. "Mmm," I murmured, unable to stem the tide of feeling which carried me away in its powerful waves. *How could I articulate this emotion?* "Oxytocin...probably also dopamine and serotonin."

He laughed a little at my awkward honesty, and I basked in the joy of listening to it echo in his chest. His laugh was my favourite sound. "Not exactly what I meant." He shifted our positions so my head was closer to his shoulder and he could see my face. "What are you thinking right now?"

"How much I love you." As trite and inexpressive as my words sounded, such a simple thing was all I could think to say.

How could this feeling be summed up by such overused words? "English is singularly lacking in the right words." I briefly pouted.

He laughed again and leaned down to kiss the top of my head.

"Móuh baahn faat yuhng yìhn yúh làih yìhng yùng ngóh deui néih ge oi." He said, making an effort enunciate each syllable clearly for my uncultured ears.

"Umm?" I asked, raising my eyebrows.

"It means 'words cannot describe my love for you'."

"So, you're saying there is a phrase for this feeling in Cantonese?"

"No. I'm saying no language has the words for this. It's numinous, mohk míng, a feeling beyond words."

His explanation only made me cry more.

"Are you alright?" He wrapped his arms around me in a wordless gesture of comfort.

"You're alive. If you want, I could fly." I didn't have the right words, so I borrowed Buttercup's, because if anyone else in the history of love had felt this, surely she had. Besides, quoting pop culture references is one of my things; it's how my brain works.

He chuckled, a deep throaty sound which produced another paroxysm of warmth from my heart. "As you wish." He winked, wearing his cocky grin and feeling pleased with himself. His look was damnably endearing.

"I know." I smirked back.

He widened his eyes in mock surprise. "Did you just Solo me?"

I grinned back in reply.

"You scoundrel," he grumbled playfully, twisting around quickly so I was pinned underneath him and couldn't escape the onslaught of ensuing tickles.

I squirmed, searching for a pillow to pummel him with. We play-fought like giddy children, chasing each other around the room until we finally collapsed on his bed, out of breath.

17

MOUNDS OF CRUMPLED paper surrounded me, their crushed white shapes forming an ocean of clouds. I lay on my stomach in the middle of my bedroom floor, stretched over my sketch board, furiously drawing Raven's new face. Thus far, the eyes and eyebrows were the only parts I had managed to get right. No matter how many times I tried, his cheekbones and nose remained elusive, as did his lips. *No, too long. Too broad. Too bulbous.* I scoured the paper forcefully with my grey eraser until my hand slipped, tearing a gash in the paper. Growling, I ripped my latest attempt free and threw it into the sea of failure. Lead filled my stomach, twisting my insides into nauseating knots.

You should have done this the moment you woke up, Riordan, not three days later. This is your own fault. Now you've lost his face forever. The loss was devastating. Without a mental image of his face, I had no soil in which to grow the seeds of my dreams; only formless clouds whose ephemeral presence evaporated under the burden of germination. The weight of evidence in favour of his continued existence was feather light on the scales of reason; the singularity of my grief was far heavier.

I struggled against the rising tide of saltwater surging against the floodwalls of my heart. The bliss of finding him had faded swiftly, replaced with a melancholy longing for the safety of his embrace. I felt the black hole in my heart begin to flare up, its familiar pull drawing me down into a desperate core of need. I knew with the wisdom of experience that my need was dangerous, capable of ensuring my own destruction. Left unchecked, this craving would pull me under the dark waves of depression, into the watery abyss of suicidal ideation. In the meantime, such need was also counterproductive. Longing told the universe I didn't have him and pushed the goal further from my reach. Knowledge alone was ineffectual against the full force of longing, however. My addiction must be sated.

I pushed the drawing board away. *Fuck it. If I can't draw his new face, I can remember the old one.* Somewhere in the recesses of my brain, my rational mind was counselling me this course of action was not wise. But that voice was too quiet, the whisper of sobriety set against the siren song of the bottle. Opening my laptop, the promise of comfort lured me into the darkness of satisfying my unquenchable desire. I carried the device to my bed, turning out the lights in favour of a strand of Christmas bulbs lining the walls. I sighed as the familiar notes of the opening song to my favourite movie began to play.

Three movies later, I was still chasing the bottom of the metaphorical bottle, seeking solace I would not find. These echoes of his past only left me hollow, serving as a constant reminder the man he had been was long dead. That specific person was never coming back, no matter how deeply I had loved him. The future we would have together would be different. He had a new face now, a new life. *Why couldn't I let go of his past?*

I knew his old face. The painful attachment to his former identity — though rooted in loss — was preferable to the discomfort of the unknown. After twenty years, my grief was a pair of comfortable, lived-in, old sweatpants, which — though falling apart at the seams — were inexplicably more comfortable than the onus of a trip to the store. The known — no matter how painful — is always more comforting than the chaotic uncertainty of the unknown. Finally, I fell asleep in a sorrow-drunken stupor, my laptop in the bed beside me evidence of my guilt.

He was waiting for me in my dreams. My excitement at seeing him was immediately overshadowed by the look on his face. His brown eyes were dark and narrowed; his jaw set firmly, full lips pinched tight. He was a caged dragon, his energy crackling around the edges. He strode back and forth in a motion too serpentine to be described as pacing. I bit my lip, uncertain. Normally, the intensity of his emotions simply smouldered in his eyes unless he deliberately chose to express them. His ability to modulate his emotions was one of the traits which had made him a talented actor in another life. His unbridled expression of emotional disturbance shocked me. Such displays were typically reserved for laughter or play. If I was seeing his emotions so clearly, he was choosing to show them to me, meaning whatever we were about to discuss was deeply meaningful to him. *No pressure*, I thought nervously.

"I'm not angry or disappointed, but we need to have difficult and honest conversation. Because I love you." I gave him credit for not using the dreaded "we need to talk" phrase, but my anxiety levels were almost as high as if he had. *This is not going to be a fun conversation.*

"It may be hurtful to you to hear this, but it needs to be said. Do you trust me enough to allow me to say it?" His draconic eyes were a blazing inferno of intensity; the once smouldering spark had ignited his entire mind.

"Yes," I replied shakily. *What else could I say?* I bit my lip again and waited, stomach churning.

He took a step forward, close enough to kiss me. Instead, he held me with his eyes. I was a gazelle caught in a dragon's gaze, powerless to look away. "Do you *want* to be with me?" he asked, his emphasis heartbreaking. I could hear the doubt in his voice. "Because this is *THE* issue which keeps us apart.

"Your beliefs make it physically impossible for me to enter your reality. As long as you hold the conviction I am dead in your world, I am. Your emotional attachment to my death has created a barrier which keeps me from being able to live in your reality." He was crying, slow, fat droplets leaking from the corners of his eyes. Each saline bead fell with the weight of a black hole, pinning me in place with precision. He needed me to see those tears, to know what my refusal was costing him.

I was crying, too. "I want to be with you more than anything else in the world." My whole world belonged to this singularity, a gravitational well I orbited in perpetual love. He was the hidden object which held my universe together, the supermassive but invisible truth my entire existence was bound to, the once-dead star who reseeded me with the alchemical components of life. *How could I want anything else? Who else would the phoenix love, if not the twice-born dragon?*

"But?" His tears were broken glass to my raw heart.

"But loving you terrifies me. You terrify me. You see me in a way no one else ever has. You expect a level of honesty and emotional intimacy which has never been part of my life before you. You hold me accountable and it's terrifying. You want me to strip myself bare of all the illusions I created to protect myself, all the lies which have ever kept me safe. In doing so, I become vulnerable to you.

"I've spent a lifetime building walls and barriers to keep myself from ever being vulnerable. At a young age, I learned vulnerability only leads to suffering. I loved my birth parents desperately. I needed them and their love. I was dependent upon them for my survival. They never loved me — I was never good enough for them no matter what I did. They judged me, yelled at me, belittled and abused me. They tore me down and tried to destroy me. Worst of all, they abandoned me. As long as I never needed anyone, I would never be hurt or abandoned again." Frightened by my honesty but unable to stop confessing, I continued shakily.

"Every brush at romance before you was a farce, a stage production designed to mimic socially accepted mores. I focused on the prettiest person in the room, picking people who would never notice me and always be the object of everyone's attention. By choosing those who could never love me back, I was safely assured of maintaining my tragic identity as unlovable and unworthy. The people who did love me — or wanted to — had picked me to pine over too. I was miserable and perfectly safe.

"Then you came along. Loving you was perfect. No-one could be more unreachable than a dead movie star. I didn't dare to love you. I only wanted to bask in your presence, nothing more. You weren't supposed to love me; that was a development I could never have foreseen, something I didn't even know how to imagine. When you did, you challenged my worldview and I couldn't handle such a crisis of self. Ultimately, I managed to make peace with the idea because you were dead. I could upgrade my tragic sense of self to the archetypal mourning lover, the eternal widow. I was safe.

"If I did fall in love with someone else, they would always pale in comparison with you. If the relationship fell apart, *when* the relationship fell apart, that outcome would be ok too, because I could always fall back on my perfect you. I never had to give anyone my whole heart or worry about normal relationship risks. You could never leave me, or cheat on me, or beat me. You could never rape me or fall in love with someone else. I had the perfect excuse to never connect with anyone or be vulnerable, while also fulfilling my need for tragedy. You might love me, but clearly the cruel universe didn't.

"You fixed that too; you found a way to come back to me, and not only come back, but come back with your memories intact. Your walk-in came with a whole new set of threats. You already know my baggage, my skeletons, my shadows, and my secrets. You know what I look like when I'm sick, fat, without makeup. You've seen me more naked than anyone else ever has, — mostly in ways that have nothing to do with clothing and everything to do with ego. You're a threat to my long-held sense of self, my concept of where I belong in the world. If my soulmate is an Adonis with a heart of gold to match, I don't get to be the tragically flawed failure or a victim anymore. If you are a dragon, I am forced to own my flames in return. Only a phoenix could be your equal. Claiming my power is terrifying.

"In all our intimacy is another threat. I've never been good enough for the people I loved before; I wasn't good enough for my birth parents. Why should I be good enough for you? Now you're possessed of the flesh again, a mortal man with every potential flaw included in the base package. If I invest all my emotional efforts and open myself up to you, what happens if you don't love me? I have spent twenty years shaping my life around the quest for you, loving you, trying desperately not to need you. What if I need you and you're not there? What if you abandon me?

"More than half my life has been shaped by your

influence; it is impossible to understand who I am without also glimpsing you. You are in my laughter, my gestures, my philosophy, my hopes and dreams. If my heart was a conch shell, your name would whisper from its depths. Loving you has made me who I am; being rejected by you would destroy me. As long as you're a dead man, I'm still safe."

I was nauseated. My impassioned monologue complete, I took several deep breaths trying to calm myself.

I held his gaze, praying the earnest honesty of my answer was enough. I wanted to puke. Self-awareness can be an ugly thing, especially when you realize you are the only thing between yourself and your heart's greatest desire. I was so terrified to need him, I pushed him away. My entire past pattern of vacillation between push and pull made perfect, sick sense. I could suddenly see all the times my unconscious had shoved the aware-ness of him away, the ten thousand ways I shrank away from the truth of his presence, terrified to admit what I truly felt. I would sooner trust the surety of *l'exquisite doeleur* I built out of longing for him than face the risk of losing him. If I didn't need him, he couldn't break my heart.

"Do you honestly think I would come back from the dead, go through all of this drama, and spend twenty years searching for you only to leave you?" He regarded me from under one quirked eyebrow, the incredulity in his voice palpable. He had a point; my fear was profoundly absurd. "I loved you when you were a selfish, angst-ridden teenager full of petulance and self-pity. What, exactly, could be so terrible about the phenomenal adult you've become that would make me love you less? Have I ever spoken or behaved in a way which would lead you to believe I'm capable of anything you've said so far?"

"No." I muttered, suppressing a flash of the petulance he mentioned. He was right; I might as well admit it. Fighting him wouldn't change anything.

"You realize this has nothing to do with me, right?"

"Yes." *Damn his insight, as always.* "This is entirely about me and my unconscious fears revolving around love and the worthiness of being loved. I'd be lying if I said I wasn't still terrified of loving you, and the intimidating levels of intimacy that entails.

"But accountability is exactly why I have to be with you, why I will find a way to make this work and believe in you, in us. You changed my life more than anyone. You loved me when I was broken and lost. Foster care may have been the best thing that could have happened to me, but at the time all I knew was it had cost me my brothers, my family, my friends, my culture... my entire worldview. I wanted to die. When my life had burned down to the ground and become nothing but ashes, you found me. You made me want to live again. Because of you I embarked on a journey of self-awareness and transformation which ultimately made me a better version of myself than I ever thought I could be. I've always loved who I am with you. You expect me to be a better person, and so I am. Even if we never find each other in the waking world, if these stolen moments are all we ever have, every heartbeat is worth it. You taught me more about love and life than anyone. Loving you made me who I am.

"And it's too late not to be vulnerable. Because I do need you; I need your love, your laughter, your tears. I need to know what you look like first thing in the morning and late at night. I need to know what you're like when you're sick — if you're a big baby or a complete grump. I need to know if you take coffee or tea, Star Trek or Star Wars, which Battlestar Galactica you thought was better, what your favourite video game is, and who you think the next Doctor should be. I need to grow old and spend the rest of my life with you, learning all the quirks and details that make you who you are. I need you more than I ever thought possible to need someone. And needing you is truly terrifying. Now I've said it." My tears were hot and salty and the pit in my stomach was about to swallow me whole, opening its gaping maw and threatening me with doom. Despite this, I held his gaze. *Why am I trembling?*

He was still crying, but his eyes had softened and a small smile played at the corners of his mouth. "Street Fighter."

"What?"

"My favourite video game is Street Fighter." He smiled.

I threw myself into his arms in relief. Burying my face in his shoulder, I took deep, shuddering breaths, inhaling and exhaling through the aftermath of impassioned panic. He held me close for several moments, allowing me to calm down before he spoke again.

"I love you. I'm proud of you for being honest with

me and for being willing to examine your unconscious beliefs. Thank you." He paused and I looked up to meet his eyes, waiting for him to continue. "What I've always loved most about you is your unconquerable will, your willingness to allow yourself to learn and grow. It's my favourite part about you." He leaned in, pausing a breath away.

"May I?"

This was my favourite part about him: after all these years and all our intimacy, he still sought my consent. His need for my blessing was his most endearing trait. In this moment I knew his constant question was a promise, a solemn vow he was worthy of my faith and would be forevermore. I suspected he had always known how skittish and feral I was. Yet he had unceasingly reached out with his gentle, patient touch, waiting for me to feel safe and learn to trust him. As much fiery passion and rage as he might possess, he banked his inferno in deference to my damage, waiting patiently for me to slowly become accustomed to the gentle heat of his flames.

"Please." His lips met mine with firm intensity, suggesting he needed reassurance as much as I did. Calm washed over my body in waves, gentle warmth replacing the cold terror I had felt.

When he stepped back, the vehemence in his eyes had returned, small sparks still burning among the coals. His voice was rich with passion. "When your desire to be with me is greater than your fear of me, we will *actually* be together. I love you."

18

THIS TIME, my conviction remained. I was filled with a fierce motivation to find answers. If I could see the big picture, I could assemble all the pieces and finally understand. Doing so would give me the clarity I needed to find peace. Hopefully, the aforementioned peace would result in finally finding him in the flesh.

Currently, I possessed too many unanswered questions concerning the circumstances surrounding our entire relationship to construct the outside frame of the puzzle, much less the inner picture. Too many pieces were missing. I decided to go back to the beginning, to the time I initially sought otherworldly help. *How does this piece fit into the larger puzzle?* Thus motivated, I sought out the Kingdom of Death.

A long time had passed since I last saw the Phantom Queen. We had not parted on the best of terms, mostly due to childish behaviour on my part. As I descended the stairs into her realm, my thoughts slipped back to my previous visit.

———

I HAD DESCENDED the stairs with purpose, feeling confident in the mythical nature of my quest. I pushed away a nagging voice, which whispered things didn't work out so well for Orpheus. *This would be different. It had to be.* At the bottom of the steps, fog rolled out of the darkness below. The sky was a dark indigo speckled with a million stars. Two flickering torches, one on either side, marked the only path forward. The Realm of the Dead possessed its own signature atmosphere, unlike any of the other realms. Normally, I loved the permanent Halloween vibe. Tonight, the otherworldly ambiance felt more ominous than usual. Much like Halloween, the Realm of Death contains the entire range of human experiences with death, as well as all our hopes and fears surrounding this rite of passage. You definitely didn't want to travel the Underworld as a horror fan; all monsters were entirely real here. Granted, I was more likely to encounter beansidhe and formori than men in hockey masks, but ancient myths are far more terrifying, having had ages to accumulate untold power. I tried not to focus on my fear, for worry of drawing any such creatures to my side, but I was truly terrified.

Just because I work for the Phantom Queen doesn't mean She can't be angry with me; She is known for Her fiery temper, after all. But I had to try to appeal to Her mercy, regardless of how angry my request might make her. As the Goddess of Death, She possessed the power to right the greatest wrong in my life and reunite me with my dead love. I stepped onto the path, committing myself to the journey. The fog swallowed me whole. Everything smelled faintly of ozone and sulphur, a strange mix of swamp and rainstorm. I wandered through the darkness, listening to the eerie silence, praying for the sound of crows to split the air. Instead, the muffled footsteps of the pack quietly padding through the fog surrounded me. I could see their dark shapes swimming in the soupy haze occasionally, a glimpse of fur and nothing more. They were painfully mute; I didn't know what to make of their silence.

The pack escorted me through the mists, herding me along the path between the dim circles of light cast by the torches. The forest around us bore the same still hush. The air was wet and heavy on my skin, and all I could do was walk, as though I were secretly under water. I pressed on, alone with the trees, the stars, and the wolves. We walked far longer than I ever remembered the path having been before. At last we came to the crossroads. The intersection stood empty.

The pack surrounded me, sitting in a circle barely beyond the edge of the fog, hulking shapes which might have been gargoyles just as easily as fur and flesh. The flapping of wings filled the air; otherwise, the murder was silent as they arrived. We stayed there, waiting for Her. *Should I call Her or should I wait?* On previous occasions, I had always arrived to find Her waiting for me. After several moments of uneasy pacing, I sat down on the ground and waited. The packed earth of the path beneath me was cold and hard, small pebbles poking into my clammy skin. *What does it mean that She isn't here yet? Is She angry with me? Have I done something unspeakably wrong? Sinned in some way? Is my being here to ask an abomination? Oh gods...* Evidently, I was meant to wait on Her. I suspected this action on Her part was a subtle reminder of my place; She was the power here, I the mere mortal.

She eventually arrived, appearing silently out of the fog. Tonight, there was only one of Her: small and dark of hair and skin, with even darker eyes. Despite Her stature, I felt as though She towered over me. *Which one is She?* I wondered. The Death Goddess I worked for wore many faces and forms, though modern witches acknowledged a central three. The textbooks always advised She be approached as a singular aspect, one face at a time. The Wiccan texts often exhorted witches to avoid Her altogether; between Her unorthodox role as a deity of sovereignty whose mere existence threatened the Wiccan classification system, Her association with creatures of Gaelic horror tales, and a host of other traits which made well-meaning Eurocentric white folk generally uncomfortable, She was a force for cognitive dissonance and ego destruction. Her wrath was also literally the stuff of Irish legend.

"Great Queen." I rose with a gesture somewhere between a bow and a curtsy.

"What is it, my daughter?" I could tell by the tone of Her voice She was aggregate Her today. *Oh boy. No pressure.*

THE LAWS OF ENTANGLEMENT

"I have come to beseech You, Mother." If She used the language of relationship, so would I. Such language was a contract between us, an acknowledgement of our mutual karmic ties. Using such language also established we each knew I was here in a personal capacity and not a formal one.

"Speak." Her tone told me She knew why I was here. I boldly met Her dark eyes with my own.

"I have come to ask for life…"

"I do not deal in life. You know this." She raised one ebony eyebrow, regarding me with a patient expression.

"But he is one of Your children, and surely his life was taken too soon. This was not supposed to be our future."

She shook Her head at me, a sad smile playing on Her rich, calla-lily lips. "Think you I know not the pain of loss?" Sorrow lined her dark features, weight pulling her face and shoulders down, burying her momentarily under a mountain of sorrow too deep to encompass. "I too have mourned. But this is not the way to ease your pain. Go ask another, the Goddess of Rebirth. She can give your love new life, but not I."

I shook my head, unable to believe I had come all this way for nothing. "Doing so would mean going through the cauldron and forgetting. Besides, he would be a child. I can't wait twenty years for him to grow up! What did we do to be cursed like this?! Why are You punishing us? Put back the wrongs done to us. Please, Mother. As Goddess of Death, only You can undo what you have done." I felt a little sick speaking to Her so impudently. However, I was Hers, of Her making, dust

207

of Her stars and woven of Her thread. I had been formed in Her image; She was my archetype. If She was angry and passionate, so was I. She made me this way. I glared at Her defiantly, eyes demanding.

My bravado quickly faded when I saw the flash of anger in Her garnet eyes. "My child, you assume too much. You imagine injustice where there is none. I took him because it was his time. Furthermore, it was his *choice.*" She narrowed Her eyes in emphasis. "He wanted to die young — he believed he would. I could not have done otherwise. He himself set these events in motion with his beliefs. He was convinced he was a tragic figure, so he became one. None of his fate is any of *my* doing. This was his destiny; he chose it himself. This was not done to punish you. It was a gift."

Her words wounded me to the core; I knew they had to be true. The Goddess of Death never lies. Why would She? The sum totality of all existence is Hers in the end. I stared at Her, tears streaming down my face. One of the crows flew to Her shoulder and cawed. She stroked under its chin with one long, sable finger. The crow contemplated me, cocking his head to the side. She returned Her gaze to me, showing equal parts amusement and frustration.

"You humans always think it's about punishment. You think the whole universe is conspiring against you, when such an idea couldn't be further from the truth. We give you exactly what you ask of us, and you curse us for giving it to you. Know this, daughter. You also chose this path. You are too angry to hear me now, but one day you will understand my words. This too was a gift. You have been given exactly what you asked for." Her smile was full of unspoken sorrow.

With this final statement She was gone — pack, murder, and all. Only the fog, torches, and forest remained. The stars no longer felt like friends; their light seemed distant and cold now. *What had She meant? How had we chosen this?! What kind of sick game was this?!* She was right about one thing: I *was* mad.

———

I RETURNED to the ever-timeless present as I continued down the stairs into the darkness below. I had changed so much since my last visit to this realm. *Will the realm have changed as well?* My understanding of the universe indicated the realm should have changed to correspond with my beliefs.

In many ways, the Underworld remained the same as always — a realm of perpetual night forever hovering in the mists of making and unmaking — pregnant with the expectation of chaos; a change barely glimpsed over the edge of the horizon. In the past, that suspense had always been the thrill of terror, a creeping sensation upon the back of my neck indicating I was being watched. Now, that anticipation was the excitement of adventure, an electric pressure raising the hairs on my arms and sounding ringing tones in my ears as my body adjusted to the changes in frequency. This was no longer the Halloween land of horror movies and night-mares, but the night of mischief and frolicking.

The crispness of autumn leaves and pine trees mixed

with the rich tang of wild soil. From the treetops, the murder heralded my approach, flying down to circle me with raucous cries of excitement. I threw the birds some crumbs and shiny trinkets, listening intently for the pack. Their happy howls had yet to reach me when one of the wolves nearly bowled me over, exuberantly wagging her tail. The rest of her pack arrived shortly thereafter, nearly knocking me down with their wet, sloppy, canine kisses. Together we walked to the crossroads, a boisterous, playful bunch.

We found the crossroads lit by torchlight, soft music coming from somewhere nearby. The music stopped short of sounding human; such things were commonplace in the Underworld. The Great Queen sat in the centre of the roads, humming to Herself. The exuberant puppy bowled into Her lap, greeting Her with kisses. She laughed in delight, hugging the wolf before standing up to greet me.

I bowed slightly. "Great Queen." Today She was any one of the ancient tribes lost to history, dark of skin and hair with piercing bright eyes. I could tell by the twinkle in Her eyes She was all of them.

"Daughter." She greeted me kindly, affection obvious in Her voice. We hugged, the exuberant pup demanding to sit on our feet while we did. It had been a long time since I had talked with Her. *Gods, I miss Her. She and this place feel so much like home*. I cried, relieved by Her familiar response instead of the formality I expected. She held me, exuding a mother's comfort, allowing me to sob on Her shoulder and unburden all my emotions until I was spent. When I was ready, She stepped back, holding my shoulders with Her rich charcoal hands. "Child?"

We sat in the road and She handed me a loom. We wove while we talked.

"I have many questions, Mother."

She laughed, throwing Her head back in the carefree manner of a child. "You always do. Inquisitiveness is one of my favourite traits. You mortals are so curious. Especially you." She tapped the tip of my nose affectionately with Her finger, Her voice ringing with amusement.

"I don't know where to start."

"Start at the beginning. Or the end. Start where your heart leads you."

"You told me once we had both chosen this."

"You did."

"But...you told me Raven placed a geas on me, yet you also said whether we live or die is ultimately up to us. So, which is it?"

She cocked Her head to the side, considering me for a moment, the crow on Her shoulder echoing Her motion. I giggled at the two of them. She smiled, raising Her head. "I believe my exact words were, 'This is bigger than the two of you'."

"But Raven said..."

"Ahh, this is a question for him then, is it not? *I* did not say it."

He wouldn't lie. Gods, like guides and spirits, sometimes withheld information: the classic faery lie. "Did you allow him to think he had?"

She smiled at me. "Clever girl. Why do you think I

did so?" She gazed at me with the avid curiosity of a chess player examining the board, wondering what their opponent's next move would be.

"It suited your purposes. You wanted him to perform an act of service in exchange for promising to keep me alive, so you allowed him to think he owed you a favour."

She nodded and smiled, narrowing Her eyes in appraisal. "Good. Continue."

"Where did he come up with the idea to do a walk-in? Non-linear reincarnation is an extremely esoteric topic. How did he suddenly come up with such a plan? Unless you suggested it. But why do such a thing?"

She raised Her eyebrows, tilting Her head to the side, Her expression conveying her expectation that I would continue.

"You wanted me alive, but you also wanted me to have hope. You're the goddess of sovereignty and trans-formation. You wanted me to evolve into a better version of myself and claim my power, which wasn't going to happen if I continued along my self-destructive path. You needed me to have a reason to hope, an idea which could inspire me to passionately pursue my path. So, you used him to prevent my suicide, while also manipulating me with my own motivations to suit your purposes. But... if we have the ultimate choice, why didn't you let me go? I thought my blood was proof I had chosen..."

"Did you strike your bargain with the clear intent to die?"

Shit. No wonder it hadn't worked. "No, I wanted to be with him."

"Exactly. *That* is the loophole I used to argue in favour of your freedom."

Loophole? Arguments? Wait, was She cosmic counsel, intervening in the celestial courts on my behalf? Shiiiit. I cocked my head to the side, examining Her for a moment. "Loophole?"

"Yes. That intent, combined with a copy of your soul agreement, was enough for the court to rule in our favour. Some of the other gods were displeased, however. I spent several favours appeasing their anger."

Favours? What kind of favours would gods trade each other?

She was my divine lawyer. The concept was simultaneously terrifying and thrilling. "Soul agreement? Wait, why am I so important to you?" Cosmic counsel implied She worked for me, not the other way around as I had always believed. How could such an idea possibly be true? If what She said about choices was true, and what Tara said about free will was also true, my soul agreement was a universally binding contract I signed with Her, which limited how the gods were able to interfere in my life. The implication was clear and cognitive dissonance-inducing: I am the ultimate authority in my life, and the cosmos is bound to help me based on the rules I specify. *Holy Shit, Batman.*

She laughed, patting me on the head like the exuberant pup. "You'll see. Go ask yourself," She said with a grin.

Clearly I wasn't getting an answer to this one. While I was here, I might as well ask her another question.

"Mother, I feel conflicted. I am driven by a need for him, which makes me feel weak. I know I should let go of my grief for his old self, but it feels like a betrayal of myself. I promised I would never let go."

She smiled, stroking my cheek like I was an infant. "In battle, one must be clear on one's priorities. You cannot have two targets; you can only focus on one thing. Choose, child. Your sorrow or your love? What do you truly want?" Her words hit my solar plexus as the truth often does, slicing through the snakeskin shell of my ego and shedding it effortlessly. I was starting to cry. I knew the answer.

"If the price of my love is vulnerability, I will gladly pay. I will strip myself bare and parade my secrets through the streets of cities. I will lay my heart and soul open for all to see if that is what is asked of me. Without hesitation."

"Then do so. Remember: your connection results in reflection. If you wish to find of him a man who remembers all you were and is committed unwaveringly to all you may yet become, you must be his match. You alone hold the answers you seek. Go find them."

I did.

19

I STOOD with my back to the wall, watching the numbers tick off the LCD screen as I descended. 10. The elevator ride was smooth. 9. My only clue to the car's motion was the flickers of light at each floor I passed. 8. *Wait. Other floors?* 7. The panel had only one button. 6. I hadn't built any other floors. 5. My brain was certain they existed, however. 4. *What's on all the other floors?* 3. *Focus, Riordan. Focus.* 2. *Deep breaths.* 1. The elevator stopped with a small lurch.

I exhaled another deep breath as the double doors opened, sliding away from the middle and into the sides. I stepped out into the cavern, checking my blind spots and sight lines as I moved. Inspecting my surroundings for ambush was an old habit — nearly archaic by now. As usual, the cavern was nearly empty, except for a large, cog-like door protected by a small military installation behind a chain-link fence. Two small garden statues stood in the sand in front of the barrier. On the left side of a small locked gate, Jizo happily smiled at me. I paused to brush off the dust and replace his worn hat. From the right, Kwan Yin beamed beatifically, offering a breath of peace with her smile. I dusted her as well and poured fresh water into her basin, lighting a stick of incense for good measure. I listened for sounds behind me, but there were none. Satisfied of my safety, I inhaled another deep breath.

My offerings made, I paused before the gate, looking up at the turrets and sentry cannons mounted above the circular door. All my defences appeared to be in working order. I opened the padlock, checking its condition. All was well. The gate didn't creak. I stepped through, walking toward the biometric scanner. I could hear the sound of motors as the sentry guns tracked my movement. I presented myself for all three scans, waiting patiently as the machine chirped in acknowledgement of each one. The final ding sounded in verification of my identity.

I turned to my right, enjoying the sound of the large hydraulics inside the door coming to life. The gear-like door slid forward with a satisfying hiss before slowly rolling to the right. I knew placing my mind palace inside a Vault was overly nerdy, but the geektastic quality made me happy. I felt a satisfying pleasure in the freedom to truly be myself.

Taking another deep, steadying breath, I stepped into the Vault, allowing my eyes to adjust to the dim interior before proceeding. I listened closely and was rewarded with the quiet metal clanking of a Mr. Handy approaching. All was as it should be.

"Good day, Madame!" Worthington greeted me in his cheerfully robotic voice, waving a metal appendage as he floated into the room on his thruster. I chuckled. He had once confessed he had chosen this particular image from my mind because it reminded him of his original form. I suspected he came from an aquatic planet and was, in fact, an adorable space squid. The cetacean playfulness he exuded always prevented him from being truly robotic. Worthington loved pretending to be a Mr. Handy, but he wasn't always convincing. I never told him, of course, finding the whole act incredibly endearing. The depth of his personality and his quirkiness were deeply reassuring in a guide. I could trust him because he loved cosplay.

"Good day, Worthington." I opened my arms in greeting.

He floated toward me and embraced me as much as his "arms" would allow. It wasn't a robotic moment, but his gesture only made me love him more.

"How can I assist you today, Madame?" He had installed extra appendages; they now totalled six. *He was a space squid.* For some reason, one of his appendages held an unlit cigar and he was wearing a bowler's hat. *Definitely endearing.*

"Is it only the two of us today, Worthington, or is Dr. Truth here?"

"She is in her office. She said when we were ready to descend she would assist us, but was otherwise occupied."

I blinked in confusion. *What does he mean?* This was the only level I was aware of building. *Descend where?*

Then again, we were talking about Dr. Truth. Of course she knew truths I didn't know about my own mind.

"Oh. I've come to get some answers, Worthington. Lead the way."

We entered a door which led into the main hallway; the metallic, futuristic sound of it closing behind me deepened my level of comfort. I imagined I could hear the Vault door outside grinding closed as well. I started to relax. Instead of branching left or right as we usually did, Worthington and I approached a set of stairs and an elevator I had never seen before. Dr. Truth was standing next to them waiting for us. She gestured to the open elevator with an outstretched arm. I followed her instructions, preceding Worthington into the shiny metal box. Dr. Truth followed, waving her hand in front of the elevator door. I didn't see any buttons or floor indicators. Otherwise, the elevator resembled a standard Vault-Tec™-issued elevator.

The car hummed quietly as we descended. *How far are we going? What is on all these levels, or is it only the two separated by layers and layers of bedrock?* My second thought gave me pause. *Levels isolated in such a manner usually indicate firebreaks, containments, or other hazards. What would my mind have placed so deeply? What would I have to face? Were we going to the lowest level?* My companions were silent, but guides often were. Navigating the Unconscious was a journey to the centre of the Labyrinth; you had to ask the right questions, no-one volunteered the answers, and the scariest things you faced would always be projections of yourself.

After a perceived eternity (not long enough for my

mind to fully wander, so probably only five to ten minutes), the car slid to a stop. We exited into a monolithic, gothic cathedral with multiple doors branching off in several directions. Dr. Truth led us directly to one such door, our muffled footsteps echoing in the cavernous space. I wished my mind had installed stained glass with lights behind it; the unbroken monotony of the architecture was beautiful, but also overwhelmingly depressing.

Producing a thick, iron ring of skeleton keys from the pocket of her lab coat, Dr. Truth proceeded to unlock the heavy oak and iron door. *What would I place behind such a massive door with such a serious lock?* I shivered a little. The door swung inward silently, and she gestured for us to proceed. We entered a brightly lit, stone room which reminded me of a treasure horde; mountains of mysterious objects filled the room. She closed the door behind us, leaving Worthington and I inside. The lock clicked and I jumped, startled. Whatever awaited me, I would have to deal with it in order to leave. *Greaaat. How comforting.* Whatever was in here, I would try to flee before it was over. *Good to know.*

In the centre of the room stood a pedestal sculpted from a material I couldn't identify. The strange substrate was luminescent, almost like glass, but warm to the touch. The pedestal crackled with static under my hands, much as an electrical device would. *Could it be a touchscreen of some kind?* I felt compelled to touch the device. I cautiously ran a finger over the surface. If this object was an electronic device, I didn't want to be too rough with it before I even knew what it did. The surface of the pedestal illuminated more as I touched it, but there was no other response. I noticed a depression in the top of the object — as though some piece of the item was missing — which would enable the whole system to work. I chuckled and shook my head. I loved it when my brain was consistent. I would leave myself this sort of puzzle. I should be grateful there was only one instead of one for each of the elements.

Worthington hovered nearby. I paused, considering my question carefully. *Use your right words.* I pictured the goblin and chuckled deeper. "Worthington, what key will unlock this puzzle?"

"The one around your neck, Madame."

I frowned, perplexed. *What key around my neck?* I pulled out my necklaces, belatedly remembering the hexagonal dog tag I wore, labelled "K.Thrace" with a symbol and a number. *Of course. Only I would leave a clue for myself which would be unlocked with Starbuck. What's inside?* I carefully removed the necklace, setting the metal charm into the depression. The console turned on, enveloping me in brilliance. For a moment, I was in the centre of a flashbang: surrounded by whiteout, the smell of ozone, and a powerful ringing sound. Heart pounding, I waited for the disorienting blindness to pass.

When I could see again, I knew I was no longer on Earth. Tears streaming down my cheeks, I knelt on the metal deck of the ship, feeling the thrum of the engines beneath me. The *hiraeth* which had been with me since childhood was instantly gone, my ancient longing for home replaced with an uncanny knowing and sense of deep relief. I knew instinctively that the home I had stared up at the stars and cried for as a child was here. My recognition centred not so much on this ship, but more so the people on it. I was home. I looked around me in awe, drinking in the holistic completion, seeking to memorize every beloved detail.

I might have stayed there forever, admiring the graceful lines of the ship, the ambient lighting, the crystals, the trees, but a group of beings I longed to join moved past. Drawn effortlessly by the gravitational pull which tethered me to them, I followed in their wake. The beings convened in a serene space I might have called a congregational chamber. The room was for meetings, I remembered. A wall-sized viewscreen looked out on a dazzling blue planet and I wept shamelessly, overwhelmed with awe for the glorious beauty of Gaia.

I have always loved Her, but this love felt more personal. As a mortal being living on Her surface, She was an abstract Mother concept, the womb which had held me for the entirety of my life. Seen from this perspective, She was both more and less; a perfect, blue sphere suspended in the infinite vacuum of space, fragile and small. Just as children must grow up to care for their parents, the tides of caregiving turning with the wheel of time, so too must our relationship with our planetary parent. A moment comes when you stop seeing Earth as a mother who exists to serve your needs and begin to see Her as a precious life, yours to protect.

The beings gathered around the viewscreen, communing. Their language existed beyond words, a telempathic melding of consciousness in which ideas passed freely from mind to mind and feelings from heart to heart. *How I missed being able to do this.* In response to my unspoken longing, one of the beings turned to meet my eyes. I had assumed — based on the lack of interaction — that I was as a ghost here, unseen and unheard. Somehow, this being seemed to sense my presence. As we stared into each other's eyes, I felt myself pulled inexorably into their depths, an invisible bungee cord returning me home. Without warning, I was looking out from the being's eyes, feeling their feelings and remembering when I had been this being. The Kara part of me was both dizzy with new sensations and stunned by emotion and the simple sense of completion I felt. For most of my life, looking into the mirror produced a vague feeling of dysphoria; the human form I wore was foreign to my true self. Looking out from behind these eyes, observing the assembled humanoid host around me, I felt unconsciously comfortable and safe in a way I never had on Earth. I knew these beings in a way which set my mind and heart at ease.

Meanwhile, the group was meeting. Watching as I was from within my own (*past?*) mind, I had access to their collective memories. Gaia had called for help from the Family of Light in transforming Herself. We were one of many groups here as a part of the mission. This meeting was a planning session for our particular group, in which each of us would volunteer to serve in the ways we were uniquely called. Each member of our group, and most of the other groups as well, was an expert in clandestine planetary missions.

We were renegades, system busters who specialized in reincarnation on various hostile planets while emissaries of a larger galactic force engaged in missions of mercy and peacekeeping. The Family of Light operated under a galactic premise recognizable to almost any Trekkie: no outside interference was allowed. Any changes to developing civilizations must occur from within. If imposed from without, any changes — no matter how well intentioned — would become tyranny. Above all else, we respected free will.

Our veneration of free will and consent left our forces in a challenging position, however. All sentient life is worthy — including planets. When a planet chooses to evolve and become what many would consider a paradise, it is the planet's inalienable, universe-given right to do so. Like all sentient beings, planets also had the right to petition the Family of Light for assistance. In order to satisfy our duty to serve planets in need of aid, while also respecting our "prime directive," we did the only thing possible — we incarnated as members of the planet's native sentient species to create change from within.

I downloaded a wealth of information from the collective memory, including mission members, details, and other technical jargon, which left my small human mind spinning. I was a kindergartener suddenly confronted with Calculus. My host, however, considered these concepts basic arithmetic.

Even with the benefit of my host's awareness and knowledge of these advanced topics, I struggled to follow the conversation. Some concepts I simply couldn't understand. Trying to wrap my mind around some of the more advanced ideas caused software conversion errors — much like opening an old Works file in a new version of Word. The text was legible, but stray lines of illegible code surrounded the message. These lines meant something to the previous software, but were indecipherable by the current. I knew they needed a volunteer for a dangerous mission: a task the group mind thought could not be done.

"I'll do it," the being formerly me said, standing up. The assembled host looked at me as though I had volunteered for a suicide mission.

"Impossible," one of the others said. "You will never make it through the density of such an entrance angle intact. Rising so quickly in frequency will require a level of acceleration unheard of amongst the species on this planet. The math shows too much possibility for failure."

"With a single member, perhaps. But two could make the journey," a second being interjected, rising quickly to their feet. The surge of pride and joy I felt from my host's heart told me my suspicions were true. If I was Starbuck, this being would be my Apollo. My would-be co-conspirator was Raven even as this being was me. The being who would become Raven drew a diagram on the viewscreen, replacing the original image of a wave with a series of interconnecting circles. The diagram rotated on its side, expanding into another dimension, resembling a double helix.

"This shape is woven into their physical structure," the being who had once been (*or would one day be*) Raven

224

continued. "We can use it for our purposes. The beings of this planet are driven by their reproductive urges, the narrow window through which they allow themselves to perceive love. If we enter the stream as partners, our shared energy vector will more than compensate for the challenges resulting from density changes. If we orbit each other at a distance of so," they expanded their arms, the diagram on the screen echoing their movement by pulling the centre of one circle to align with the perimeter of the next, "our gravitational pull will ensure a steady force we can use to slingshot up in rungs of vibration. We'll spin up these perspectives in units of seven to match their base frequency. On the seventh rotation, we will have completed one full turn, creating a hypersphere seed."

I watched as the screen resolved into a dazzling array of fourth-dimensional spheres in a pattern which reminded me of cell division on a galactic scale. I understood the language they were using, but the words made little sense. I could barely wrap my human mind around the geometry of a tesseract, much less interconnected hyperspheres. *Entry vectors? Density changes? Gravitational orbits and energetic slingshots? It sounded like they were planning an FTL jump off the known charts, not talking about Earth. Unless...* The sequence of Kara Thrace at the controls of the Galactica's FTL console flooded my memory, the song she alone heard. On some strange, instinctual level, I understood.

A certain harmonic frequency needed to be reached. This being who had been (*or would be*) me was volunteering to be one of the carriers of the harmonic code.

They would bear the resonance, transporting it to Earth and altering the planetary energy grid to match. The technical details of how exactly they (*we?*) would accomplish this tonal modulation were part of the coding my limited understanding failed to translate. My only context clues were: the process had to do with my empathy and the specific crystalline composition of Earth. How these resulted in shifting planetary harmonics I was left to guess. I only understood my particular tone or set of frequencies was an integral part of the global transformation process; it would help Her ascend. I may not have fully understood the concept, but even a glimpse was enough to be profound. Raven and I made a promise to each other long ago (*or would, long from now*), to carry a message from the stars to the children of Earth. This sounded preposterous to my current self, but my host — or Starbuck as I was coming to call them — was deeply invested. As unlikely and irrational as the whole concept sounded, the truth of my realization resonated in the shared body of my host, and in my distant own. I felt this knowing as indelible truth, my inner compass striking north with emotional precision. My mind might try to deny or dismiss this idea, which dwarfed its small Homo sapiens understanding, but my body was equipped with instinc-tive energy awareness that unfailingly detected the truth, no matter how painful or cognitive-dissonance inducing truth might be. The seriousness in this room was entirely appropriate to a tactical council working to ensure the future of the universe.

One by one, others in the group volunteered to go

with us, each carrying part of the frequency. Our mission was too important to send anyone alone, so we went in pairs. Each pair had a plan to get the frequency through the density of the planet. Some members of the group I recognized as people I knew and loved "now" as Kara: Thor, Cobra Lay-dee, Rhiannon. I knew I hadn't met others in the group yet in my current life, but I recognized them with the familiarity of the heart. Slowly, the room faded, dissolving the way dreams often do.

20

I FOUND myself standing at the console, crying. I crumpled at the knees and sat on the floor, head in my hands. Huge waves of cognitive dissonance washed over me, remnants of childhood "re-education." I warred with my emotions, my rational mind flinging ammunition with the panic of a force under siege. Sequences of images flashed across my mind's inner eye.

I WAS STANDING in my crib, leaning against the dark, wooden siderail as I reached to be picked up. Several strands of white hair were clutched in my hand as I cried inconsolably, yelling at the top of my tiny lungs. "Tate me!!! Tate me!!!" I pleaded, even as my true parents smiled sadly and disappeared. I screamed bloody murder then, crying and wailing with all the force of a broken heart. *How could they leave me? What did*

I do? Why did they leave me here? Why couldn't I go home with them? Was I bad? Did they not love me anymore?

I LAY awake next to a sleeping adult, one of the human parents assigned to me. I had yet to adapt to the food of this world, and I could not sleep when I was hungry. I reached my small hand to her throat, placing it on the hollow of her neck. I sighed softly as the energy of her body fed into the vortex of my palm, filling me. They believed I slept with them at age five because I was scared of the dark. Truthfully, I didn't want to starve to death.

MY SMALL NOSE was pressed against the wire glass window of my hospital room, watching the night nurses go about their shifts. I counted to ten, waiting for Nurse Johnson to return to the station and start drinking her coffee. I slipped my door open, slowly sliding through the dark hallway and into the room across from mine. I ran my fingers along the edges of the board games in the dark, searching for the bookshelves. *One, two, three — there!* My fingers found the next set of shelves. I began pulling down books, shoving them into the hem of my hospital gown, using it as a makeshift bag. I had grabbed almost as many as I could carry when the fluorescent light turned on, blinding me. Behind me, I could hear a nurse clearing her throat. It was Nurse Wythe, the one who reminded me of Mathilda's Trunchbull. *I'm in for it now.*

"What are you doing?! You know you're not allowed in the playroom! Put those down, right this instant!" Her imposing form blocked the doorway, my only exit.

"But I finished the other ones, and I don't have anything else to read. I waited until the other kids were in bed. I won't get them sick this way. Nurse Stevens said I could borrow the books as long as I brought them back. But she didn't come to work today."

"Enough! Put those down and march your butt back to your room right now, young lady or I'm calling security on you. I should've known a kid like you would try to steal. Shame on you! Stealing from sick children." She jabbed her white finger in the air repeatedly as she pointed at me.

"But I wasn't..." I tried to argue, but was stopped by a sudden smack across my mouth. My eyes watered with the sting. It wasn't anything compared to what I usually received at home; if she thought I would cry, she was wrong. I narrowed my eyes and glared.

"Get. In. Your. Bed. Now." She spoke as if each word were a separate sentence, ripping the books out of my hands and grabbing me roughly. She forcibly turned me around and began marching me to my room. "From now on, you are confined to your room. You will not leave, period. I'm calling Doctor Jones and recommending you be moved to a state facility. They're equipped to deal with crazy children like you. You don't belong here with children who are actually sick. I hope they give you a padded cell, a straightjacket, and more rounds of electric shocks. A little monster like you deserves no less." She spat the words at me as though I were a bitter taste she could not wait to be rid of, spittle landing on my face. The door slammed shut behind me, and I heard the key turning in the lock. I walked to the window and stared down at the city lights below me, wondering how strong the glass was and if I would die jumping from this height.

Accept their reality and get my freedom back. Persist in seeing things no one else can see, hearing things no-one else can hear, and insisting I'm not from here and stay locked in prison forever. Neither seemed like a viable option. Honestly, I would rather die.

A blue-white light appeared in the glass, a reflection of the doorway behind me. I turned quickly, thinking a nurse had returned, fearing another dose of Thorazine. Last time it had been an injection; those couldn't be hidden in the back of my mouth. Instead, I saw only the light. No hallway, no nurse's station, no hospital. Curious, I walked into it, entering a brightly illuminated hallway. The smell of ozone permeated the air, and I was filled with sudden elation.

They had come back for me! They were here to save me! I smiled so broadly my face hurt and I found myself running through the next doorway, eager to see my family again. I threw myself at the being in the room beyond, embracing them, crying. I clutched at the garments they wore, sobbing my heart out.

"Thank you, thank you, thank you! Thank you for coming back for me! I knew you were coming back! Can we go home now?" Seeking reassurance, I looked up into their face.

Instead I found a sad smile. "I am so sorry, dear one. This is not what we wanted for you. But your memories are too dangerous for you now. They have already begun to study you. Even now, there are those in your government seeking children such as yourself for experiments. We cannot allow them to have you. It pains us to do this, but we must block your memories for your own good. They will return to you when you need them most." They placed their extra-long digits over my face.

When I woke the next morning, my memories were gone. The doctors, convinced the injections and shocks had worked, sent me home with a bottle of pills.

I RETURNED TO THE PRESENT, the segmented parts of my personality at war with one another. My inner child was crying with the profound relief of recognition. A wordless sense of homecoming washed over me in waves as tensions I hadn't known I carried were released. Even as I relaxed into the acceptance of self, my survival mind was screaming.

This is crazy. You are not an alien. It's not true. It can't be. They'll take you back to the hospital and give you injections and electric shocks again. You are crazy. This is not real. This is a product of trauma. Your mind invented a family who loved you because you couldn't handle your childhood. You needed to believe you were adopted, that you weren't from here, because it meant you had a magical home and family to go to.

Ironically, the appeal to logic introduced a new factor to my internal debate. I stepped back from the two emotional sides of my brain and considered their respective evidence. *If the seemingly bizarre circumstances I recently re-witnessed were not in fact real, why was I so relieved to find them? Moreover, how much did sanity truly matter?* In terms of practical application, psychology is about identifying maladaptive behaviours and beliefs. While my extra-terrestrial backstory might technically be crazy viewed through the lens of society's camera, this story is mine. *If denying my stellar origins caused so much pain and suffering, wasn't denial itself maladaptive? If acceptance brings me peace of mind, isn't acceptance the path to healing?* My rational mind didn't have an answer. *Is this why I would flee the room, or does the truth only grow more uncomfortable from here?*

I came here to learn why I chose a dead soulmate instead of some other, saner course. *Conventional ideas of reality be damned. What about my experiences with the gods?* So much of myself and my experiences are inexplicable to Muggles; once I have been made safe for Muggle minds, I am no longer me. In my obsessive pursuit of performative normalcy, I limited myself with the same abusive, autocratic hegemony my birth parents practiced. Their fear of me sent me to the hospital for observation. I had read my psychiatric file: "Mother says child either possesses magical powers or is schizophrenic." *Thanks, birthmonster.*

Because my human birth parents had viewed my gifts as burdens and had loved me less than I needed, I spent a lifetime doubting myself, hiding my true self from everyone around me in fear. I was afraid my essence rendered me unlovable; I was a cursed monster unworthy of love. I hid my light, smothering my spark in response to societal conditioning. It made me miserable. Whether the abuser is external or a facet of yourself, limiting yourself never comes without dire emotional consequences. Of course I had been suicidal. Who wants to live trapped in a lie? In order to make peace with myself, I had to accept all of me with equanimity. I needed to let go of judgement and allow myself to be exactly who I was.

I had spent a lifetime denying my truth. I pretended to be human; I tried desperately to be normal. I tried to be "good:" to slavishly follow the arbitrary societally created rules to the point of obsessive perfection. It only brought me ruin. Granted, I now saw it as a ruin which birthed the magic of my new life from the ashes of the old one. What I had once perceived as the worst day of my life — the day the sheriff and a social worker showed up to take me away — had actually been my genesis. Ending or beginning was simply a matter of perspective. The trauma of my past led me to my sister and my **real** family. Ruin led me to practicing magic and learning to use my gifts again. Ruin led me to Raven.

In turn, Raven had led me to myself. The epic journey I had undertaken to confront the gods themselves ultimately led me to confront myself and learn I had chosen this course. My path was part of a brilliant plan I had (*would have?*) to save myself, and in doing so empower and inspire the rest of the world to save themselves as well. *But how? And why?* I wanted so badly to fully understand.

The robotic clanking sounds of my Mr. Handy reached into my reverie, reminding me I didn't have to face this alone. *If I'm an alien... who are the gods? Where do they come in?*

"Worthington, who are the gods?"

"In what respect, Madame? Please clarify your question."

"In relationship to me, what role do they play in my life? How are they involved in this?"

"They are facilitators, those who were once incarnated in a physical form but have chosen to focus their time and energy on assisting the living."

"They're ascended humans."

"They are ascended *beings*, Madame." His emphasis gave me pause.

"Some of them are also aliens?"

"We do not use the word *alien*. They are all members of the Family of Light, as you are. Our identities are not so tied to our physical forms or planets of existence as human identities are. There is no difference between us. We are all family."

"So... who works for whom? Do I work for them, or do they work for me?"

"Neither, Madame. You are all in the greater service of Light. They are here as assistants, to facilitate the communication of ideas and transmission of energy. They can access resources currently unavailable to you and bring you answers and information you need." He made a mechanical hissing sound, almost a sigh. "Imagine physical incarnation as a boarding school, a college where stellar children come to learn, grow, and have the experiences of the flesh. The gods are slightly more experienced and have been given the responsibility of empowering your learning journey. They are your parents, your teachers, your counsellors. They are here to support, assist, and encourage. However, they are bound by the laws of free will and can only assist as much as you allow them."

"Oh. But..." I thought back to the results of my ritual, and the Phantom Queen's statements about courts and arguments. "They don't always agree on how best to help us?"

"They remain individuals with free will. They have their own opinions, as do you. Ascended does not mean they are without personality, Madame. In cases of disagreement, the gods will meet and discuss what actions best assist an individual in the completion of their soul agreement."

"How do they determine which god has the best interpretation?"

"As in human families, some members are more closely related than others, Madame. In these cases, the parent-gods — or those who share vibrational frequencies with the individual — are allowed to speak on the individual's behalf. Because they originate from the same source, they are best suited to understand and communicate the true desires of the oversoul."

"Oh." *Well, that explains that, at least.* The eternally curious Ravenclaw part of my brain had ten thousand more questions to ask. I could spend hours asking Worthington to explain the mechanics of the universe. But an eternity of asking questions wouldn't bring me any closer to Raven or to leaving this room. I frowned, refocusing on the task at hand.

"Worthington, who is Raven to me?"

"In what respect, Madame?"

"In the soul-map, Worthington. In the plan." I hoped my explanation was specific enough to receive an answer to my question.

"He is your key."

Was that the wrong question? Too late now. I chuckled at myself, feeling fractionally better. "In what respect, Worthington?" If nothing else, I liked the symmetry of the question. Maybe, my phrasing was clever enough to merit further explanation.

"Who were you before his arrival in your life, Madame?"

He answered my question with a question — how Zen. I gazed at the ceiling, considering the angry, bitter teenager who hated the world because she was convinced she was a monster unworthy of love. All the magical knowledge I acquired in my epic quest to reunite with Raven was alchemical knowledge about myself. I had laboured so long under the delusion that my quest was about finding him, I had entirely failed to realize it was I who was lost.

The word for this feeling in Zen Buddhism is *satori*. The dawning of light in my heart and mind were the flames of rebirth, the cosmic gateway between the darkness and the light, where all one has been is suddenly gone and all one will yet be is a mystery. The light of transformation began to escape my core, and it rippled out of my aura in a borealis of fire. I was a phoenix. I felt an orphic frisson sweep out from my heart; I had become the ace of cups in Rhiannon's tarot deck, love and self-acceptance rippling out in glorious waves.

I had never been cursed. I had always been a renegade, a virago. I had chosen the challenge of self-knowledge in a glorious act of love, a ritual of worship dedicated to the beauty of all that is. In this moment, I finally understood the Words of the Star Goddess: "all acts of love and pleasure are my rituals." In recognizing the exultant divinity of myself, I gave praise to the universe for creating me. I had been singularly blessed with a partner as committed to self-exploration as I was, so committed he had given his life to be exactly what I needed when I needed him most. My quest to bring him to me brought me to myself. Even if we never reunited, ours was still the most beautiful love story I had ever heard. I wept with recognition of how blessed I was, how grateful I felt to be his partner on this wild journey.

Behind me, the lock clicked open, even though the room contained more to explore. Shelves lined the walls, each horizontal surface packed full of books and scrolls. Chests overflowed with treasure. Maps of long-lost lands competed with paintings, wall scrolls, and a mural. A floor-length tapestry hung on one wall, its radiant rendition of a dragon and phoenix in flight faintly glowing with magic. This room *was* a treasure hoard, one more suited to the final dungeon of a campaign than my mind. My mind belongs to a game master, however. In hindsight, this room was perfect. I left myself a treasure at the end of the quest I planned for fun and transformation. *Of course.* I smiled. *Now, to find out what was in here.*

"Worthington, what is all this?"

"All of what, Madame?" *Riiiiight. Not specific enough.*

I gestured to the room, indicating the treasure trove yet to be explored. "THIS."

"More, Madame."

"In what respect, Worthington?" My sass knew no bounds.

If robots could sigh, Worthington would have. *Ah, my silly space squid. How I love you.* "In all the ways which you are now aware, Madame. They represent the aggregate sum of lessons learned in lives across the multiverse. They are the echoes in your pond. These are the collected treasures of your lives, with and without Master Raven."

"Without?" *Master Raven, how cute. I might have to start calling him that.*

"Yes, Madame. Without."

I sighed. "In what respect, Worthington?" I tried in vain to keep the frustration out of my voice, but I rocked my head back and forth like a pendulum.

"Non-incarnate as a physical being in the realm you now occupy." I swore his tone was dry and cutting. *Touché.*

"I'm guessing we don't get a lot of happy endings." *Surely there was more than beautiful tragedy in this plan, right?*

"Not often, Madame. However, when you do receive a 'happy ending,' as you so say, the force of your gravitational attraction reshapes worlds. All is as it should be, as the two of you designed. This is the promise of your love: a vow of perpetual sacrifice on the altar of self-examination, toward the greater goal of enlightenment. Should the two of you arrive at your pinnacle together, you possess the power to accomplish dramatic evolutionary leaps. You have become something of a legend."

"A legend?" I laughed. This whole conversation began so far outside of my comfort zone; my understanding of the universe was expanding exponentially. The amount of growth required was incredibly painful; cognitive dissonance often is. Most humans are hydrophobic felines when faced with cognitive dissonance. I usually drank it by the barrel; now I was swimming in it.

"I believe you have heard some of them, Madame. You might perhaps use the word archetype." Apparently, Worthington was also a smartass.

I was tempted to ask him in what respect, but that would likely result in a lecture on how mythology functioned. I would have enjoyed such a conversation more with Joseph Campbell. "Cite a reference material which exists outside this room, Worthington." *Surely, no-one could be writing this because no one else knew.*

"Isis and Osiris. Ka Suo and Li Luo. Orpheus and Eurydice. Chay-Ara and Khufu. Takeshi and Quellcrist, Wesley and Buttercup, Moirin and Bao. Reference your popular culture, Madame. I believe you will find you are an archetype and have been throughout many cultures and times. The tale of the lovers who refuse to allow death to separate them has been around for quite some time."

"Are you saying those are all my lives?" I asked.

"They are your ripples, Madame. Are you the photographs taken of you? An image is a representation of an object, not always the object itself. In your world, photographs serve as evidence of the existence of said object, do they not? Behold your evidence." He gestured with a metal appendage, indicating the treasure piled around us.

I was blown away by the concept of being an archetype, but I wasn't entirely reassured. *Is my quest doomed to failure? Is this one of the lifetimes without? Is this a tragedy, or not?*

"Is this all a ruse, Worthington? Did I create this love for myself to achieve mastery and still be alone? Is this all we will ever have?"

Worthington beeped a series of "does not compute" beeps. It made him sound like R2-D2. Normally, I adored it. In this moment, I felt frustrated by it. *Remember the Labyrinth, Riordan. What question **aren't** you asking?*

I wouldn't have chosen this course solely to torture myself. On the other hand, I knew myself well enough to know I was incontrovertibly a tactical thinker who would risk everything on a crazy, big, impossible win. *With and without. Circles. Completion and emptiness. What had Apollo/Raven said about cycles of seven?*

"Worthington, what is the difference between the lives with and the lives without?" I was pleased with myself, imagining the cartoon lightbulb illuminating above my head.

The gears clicked and whirred while he processed my question. I imagined it was the sound of him thinking. "The living person persists in loving. They are transformed by love, transferring larger amounts of their ultimate consciousness into their physical form. I believe some of your philosophies call this the pursuit of enlightenment or self-actualization. This practice allows them to choose from a greater number of realities." He projected a green hologram into the air between us, astromech droid style. *I didn't know he could do that!*

"If x is the total number of all possible outcomes, it is confined by a matrix of parameters determined by the set of agreements an individual holds as the result of their personal, inherited, and cultural beliefs. Examination of the self allows one to pinpoint those equations which determine the overall scope of the matrix, altering the possible variables and expanding its possible answer set. The fewer the constraints placed upon the matrix, the closer its potential number set approaches to infinity. At that point, all outcomes are possible." He projected the math onto the screen as he spoke, and I could clearly see what he meant. The linear algebra of souls was beautiful stuff.

"You're saying we essentially use our love as a gravitational slingshot, borrowing and accelerating each other's momentum to achieve incredible speeds? Sometimes we crash and burn and sometimes we explore the galaxy?"

He chirped affirmatively. "An excellent metaphor, Madame. I see my visual aids were effective."

"Yes, thank you, Worthington. You said, 'the living person.' What is different in the "with" lives with regard to the non-living partner?"

"They acquire a new matrix of possibilities." *Of course. Ask a better question, Riordan.*

"Ok, so they reincarnate. But sometimes rebirth doesn't go forward and backward. Sometimes reincarnation goes sideways?" Trying to translate the math into three-dimensional terms was compressing its own matrix of possibilities. *Is this how dimensions work? Oh, of course it is!* Another lightbulb brightened above my head in my imagination.

"Your question is based upon a false assumption of time. Time is not as you perceive it to be, Madame. All of time exists as separate moments, all at once. Imagine time — as you perceive it — is a series of photographs, taken second by second as in time-lapse photography. Put the moments together into an animation or a "flip book," and linear, sequential time appears. However, all the photographs exist together in the same space, do they not?"

The projector reappeared, math filling the air between us. He continued to lecture. "If infinity contains all that is, each dimension is limited by the amount of infinity it can include. 'Higher vibrational frequencies' are simply larger containers. Like lives, each dimensional reality can only hold so much of the available information packet. No one container can ever be large enough. The eternal being you would recognize as you is much larger than your container can possibly hold. Much like trying to fit one of your gallons of water into a single drinking glass, it would not fit."

The projector turned off. "There is more of you than can be contained by flesh, Madame. I believe your scientists are now calling it 'nonlocal consciousness.' All your lifetimes exist at once."

Ok. We are all living multiple lives at once but are only aware of one. This didn't explain *how* walk-ins work or why we weren't all reincarnating in such a manner. "What is different about what Raven did this time than what is normally done?"

"When a soul is incarnated in physical form, energy collects around the soul from the soul's interactions with others. What you perceive of as 'this you,' or 'Kara' is the sum of your interactions in this life. I believe some of your philosophies call this effect karma. Upon death, this energy dissipates back into the greater whole of 'higher self.' The more well known a person is, the larger their karmic envelope. The longer they are remembered as that identity after death, the longer the energy maintains a unique, separate identity from the greater whole of the self.

"A stronger concentration of a substance will colour a larger body of water. Raven's exit packet was suffi-cient to colour his energy stream. The energy from his tragic death and mourning fans fed the strength of his former identity. Also, the energy of your love fed into his energy. Raven only needed a parallel life he was already living in order to expand his matrix enough through conscious choice or trauma to receive his energy packet. The other self could, through focused affinity, connect with his source energy and download more of the Raven packet until his highest evolved awareness is as fully present as the human body will allow."

"But?" I sensed this quantum math problem had more variables than I realized. *What had Raven said about me not allowing him to be alive? How do I get to the castle at the centre of the Labyrinth?*

"The Raven packet is so large it can only fit into the higher dimensions, which requires you to also be in a higher dimension, and to also have the packet which states he is alive. As long as your cords to him are coded with the matrix of who he was before, you limit yourself to the realities in which he is dead. In order to coexist, your matrix must share base formulae with his."

"Which is why we so rarely manage to succeed. Our success is the inevitable statistical anomaly." *How crazy is my original plan if this is the best fix?* "Which kind of life do you think this one is, Worthington?"

"Which kind do you want it to be, Madame?"

EPILOGUE

I SIT BEHIND MY TABLE, my heart beating a staccato rhythm in my throat, the edges of my eyes prickling with unshed tears. Reaching for my glass, I take a deep drink of water, focusing on the precise row of metallic pens, the straight lines of my neatly-stacked books, the edges of my portfolio case.

What if no-one comes by my table? What if they hate how simple my cover design was? What if they realize the story is true and called a psychiatrist? *Calm down, Riordan. Don't think; feel. Get out of your head and into the totality of the now.* Setting down my glass, I breathe into my gut and out as slowly as I can, settling into rhythm of the calming square. Five in, five pause, five out, five pause. Repeat. Waves of calm wash over me, my heart rate slowing in response to my breath as the first person enters the dealer's room.

As it turns out, I needn't have worried. I am so busy talking to people that I don't even have time to eat.

Sometime in the early afternoon I reach under my table, pulling out another stack of sleek black books to refresh my rapidly dwindling pile. I feel momentarily overwhelmed with sheer joy and gratitude for having sold any copies of my first book, much less so many. As I expand my focus into my body, my heart skips several beats, accelerating at Autobahn speeds. Time slows around me, until my every breath is an eternity. In front of my table, someone clears their throat.

I straighten my book pile and sit up, raising my head and smiling at my latest visitor in greeting. The fabric of reality around me distorts in an infinite dolly zoom of compression. I freeze, unable to breathe or move, my entire being centred on the person standing opposite me. I know the finely sculpted lines of those cheekbones, the long nose and full lips. My stomach muscles contract as I force myself to breathe.

"I was wondering if you would sign my book?" He reaches toward me, a copy of my novel clutched in his long tawny fingers. I notice the edges were worn, the spine cracked and creased, the bottom corner of the front cover curled up slightly.

"Of course." I accept the book, blinking furiously as the red thread on the cover blurs slightly. I reach for a pen and open the cover, taking another deep breath to steady myself and focus on the present. "Who should I make it out to?"

"Raven."

My heart skips another beat.

I pause, my hand above the book, reminding myself once more to breathe. *Dear Gods, what do I write?* There is already a dedication to him in Chinese, after all. *Breathe, Riordan. Write something, anything.* I take another deep, steadying breath and finally write, "To Raven. Thank you. All my love, Kara Riordan."

I hand the book back to him, daring to make and keep eye contact as my heart continues to race. We hold onto the book together far longer than normal, each reluctant to let go. We might have stood there for even longer, staring at each other awkwardly over the cover of my memoir, but my stomach growls loudly, interrupting an otherwise potentially perfect moment. I blush, laughing a little, and let go of the book.

His mouth curves into a broad grin, golden-brown eyes twinkling in amusement as he holds out his hand. "May I have the honour of accompanying you to lunch?"

"Please."

The End

Review it now!

NOTES

Chapter 3

1. Jeanette Winterson, *Sexing the Cherry* (Vintage: 1990), 80.

Chapter 4

1. The Dust Brothers, *This is Your Life*. Restless Records. MP3. 1999.

ABOUT THE AUTHOR

Maya Preisler attended UNC Charlotte for a BFA in cross-disciplinary studies with a minor in International Studies. She is the illustrator of a book series helping children navigate foster, kinship, and adoption care. A survivor of childhood trauma, she aged out of the foster care system and was adopted as an adult. When she's not writing or creating art, she can be found working on her latest cosplay or saving Gaia and preventing the apocalypse. Find out more at www.mayapreisler.com

www.ingramcontent.com/pod-product-compliance
Lightning Source LLC
Chambersburg PA
CBHW020747250626
47155CB00003B/957